THE MAN
IN THE DARK

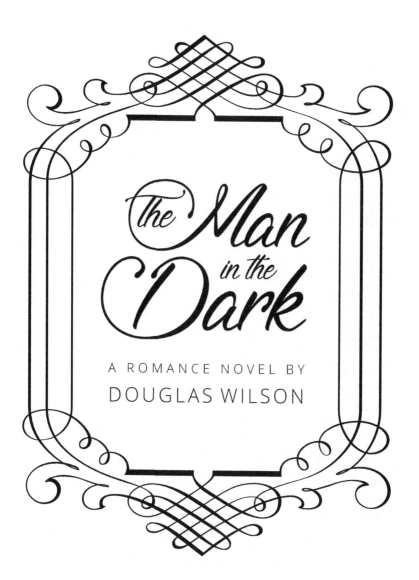

the Man in the Dark

A ROMANCE NOVEL BY

DOUGLAS WILSON

Douglas Wilson, *The Man in the Dark*
Copyright © 2019 by Douglas Wilson

Published by Canon Press
P. O. Box 8729, Moscow, Idaho 83843
800-488-2034 | www.canonpress.com

Cover detail images "Idaho Street, Looking East—Weiser, Idaho" from
Cardboard America (cardboardamerica.org). Used by permission.

Cover design by James Engerbretson
Interior design by Valerie Anne Bost
Printed in the United States of America

Library of Congress Cataloging-in-Publication Data forthcoming

19 20 21 22 23 24 25 26   10 9 8 7 6 5 4 3 2 1

Of course I could not write a romance novel
without dedicating it to Nancy,
even though I have dedicated other books to her.
To be clear,
I would have to write a million books
to be even kind of even.

CONTENTS

SAVANNAH WESTMORELAND

Thou art beautiful, O my love, as Tirzah,
comely as Jerusalem, terrible as an army with banners.
SONG OF SONGS 6:4

One solitary mountain sat about five miles north-east of the small town of Paradise Valley. It was a short ridge with modest ambitions, covered with pine, and did not really tower over anything, but when you looked at it directly you saw that it *was* in fact a mountain. The town below it was situated on rolling hills, rich with grain, and the late summer breeze meant that the golden hills were swirling with a stationary yet

1

mildly agitated activity. It looked just like mischievous whirling spirits were running up and down the hills, and perhaps they were.

A young woman stood looking out at the distant grain—stalks moving in obedience to their invisible authorities. It was Sunday morning, and Savannah Westmoreland was walking to church a little early to avoid making that trek after the heat had become a bit more troublesome. She turned away from watching the grain, somewhat reluctantly, cast a few glances over her shoulder, and started off. The walk home after church would be hot, but at least it would all be downhill.

Savannah had first tried the Presbyterian church on the hill on the eastern edge of town when she had arrived in town five years before, had loved it, and had been making that same walk ever since. She had felt a little bad about her instant loyalty to just one church, because she had always intended to try the others, but she had never gotten around to it. She was very happy right where she was—happy with everything, that is, except for the loss of their dear pastor the previous winter. He had been a wise and good shepherd, but then, like a character right out of Genesis, he had been found to be full of years. One night at prayer meeting—Savannah had been there at that meeting—he told everyone that it was time to follow his Emma, and late that night he was gathered to his people, also as in Genesis. Emma, his wife of forty years, had died two years before.

And this was now the second Sunday since the arrival of their new pastor, the Rev. Thomas Goforth.

Savannah was looking forward to hearing him preach again, even though his first venture last Sunday had been more . . . *interesting* than edifying. He was a tall, good-looking man, with black hair parted in the middle, and he had quite a good pulpit presence. He had begun very well, and seemed quite assured of his text. But about five minutes into the message, Savannah had looked down for just a moment at her handbag, and it seemed that at just that second, he had somehow lost the center. The sermon began mysteriously to meander, and though many good things were still said, they all seemed like pearls rolling around on a table without any thread to make them into a necklace. Although it was not *terrible*, Savannah had still been a little bit embarrassed for him. And since she deeply hated being embarrassed for other people in that kind of way, she had departed for home that first Sunday through the side door. And this was why she had not yet met Pastor Thomas at the back of the sanctuary the way almost everyone else had done.

But she was looking forward to meeting him this Sunday. For some reason, she had come to assume that last week had simply been a case of the first sermon jitters and that everything this week would be quite naturally improved.

As, in fact, it was. This week was quite different. When he first ascended into the pulpit this time, Savannah noticed that his aquiline nose was slightly bent to the right, as if it had been broken in a football game or a boxing match. As she found out later, it had in fact been both—the football game taking it to the left, and the boxing match moving it back to the right and a little farther over.

He began his message, this second message, in a very composed frame, and while he did warm to his subject, it was not without ministerial dignity, and he also finished composed. The pearls were still there, and the thread was now there. Now *that* was a necklace. Most important to Savannah was that he was coherent throughout. In her daily task of teaching school, she was fierce with her high school students about coherence. With her students, she could insist on it, and because she was a good teacher, she could usually make it happen. When her peers were incoherent, there was nothing she could do but feel embarrassed for them, which she hated.

But whatever had happened the previous week did not happen this time, and everyone in the congregation of about one hundred saints was quite content. She would have no trouble this week going out the main door, looking her new minister straight in the eye, shaking his hand, greeting him, and welcoming him into their warm little community. And after the final *amen*, and visiting with her friends for twenty minutes, that is exactly what she did.

However, as she did so, coming close enough to him to shake his hand, she felt like she was in the presence of someone . . . formidable somehow. She wasn't sure she liked that. And she was also just as sure she did like it. And he was taller than she had thought.

"Welcome to Paradise," she said. She quickly intro-
duced herself, made a few comments about the heat,
school-teaching, and the sermon, in that order, and then
moved out to the street with all appropriate decorum.

He had greeted her warmly, but no more warmly
than the Widow Gooch right in front of her and Mr.
Parsons the wheat farmer just behind. But as she turned
left at the bottom of the stairs to return by her usual
route to her boardinghouse, which was just down 3rd
Street, she noticed that right behind Mr. Parsons was
Mr. Lambeth, the banker.

Mr. Lambeth. He was the only suitor she had ever
had in this town, and it had taken three painful visits,
each one of them increasingly awkward, to persuade
him to rejoin the ranks of all those who were not her suit-
ors. He had been quite persistent, and quite displeased
at his lack of success. He was not at all used to being told
no. He had moved out to the Pacific Northwest several
years before—from Delaware, she thought—and he had
not moved out west in order to have his will crossed.
He had big plans, extensive abilities, and an ambition
to match. Things usually went his way at the bank, and
the tellers were all terrified of him, but Savannah wasn't
there at the bank. She had been singularly uncooperative in his campaign for romantic conquest. If pressed
for her reasons by a friend, she would have said nothing. She would have told herself that she didn't like the
shape of his head, but there was more to it than that.

Lambeth was a sturdy man, but by no means fat.
His brown hair was longer on top, and cropped closely

at the sides. He had small ears, but not absurdly small. He was not unattractive, but he wasn't really attractive either. He was an inch or two taller than Savannah. She had nothing against his looks, but his looks didn't exactly present any strong counterarguments against the "not Lambeth" sentiment that had taken a deep root in Savannah.

So now Mr. Lambeth shook the hand of the new minister firmly, but from what Savannah could see in just a brief moment, both men looked wary. They were each circling the other without actually doing so. "Reverend," Lambeth said. The new minister grinned in return. "On my good days," he said. "Intermittently reverend on the others."

Savannah looked away, wondering what might come of all *that*, and headed back home to her room at Mrs. Fuller's. Mrs. Fuller ran a boardinghouse that was straight across the street from the mechanical shop that tended to the town's cars, all twenty of them.

Mrs. Fuller owned one of those cars, and from time to time she let Savannah take it out. But Savannah did not abuse the privilege—she would only ask to borrow it a couple times in a year. She had once found a place outside of town where she would drive the car, park it, walk up a small hill she had discovered that had a glorious prospect to the south. There she would look at the hills, and pray and cry.

The people at church thought her the most marriageable woman they knew—especially all the women thought it—and she knew what they could not know, which was that her prospects for a real Christian marriage were as slim as they could possibly be. But her time on that hill was the only time she ever allowed herself to think at all about her time in Milwaukee, and apart from these occasional visits to the hill she was, for the most part, honestly and consistently cheerful.

She came to herself and found she was at the foot of her front steps, and not back on her hill at all. She shook herself out of her melancholy reverie, which was surprising for being a little out of place, and began to walk slowly up the steps. "Dinner is on, dearie!" Mrs. Fuller said out the window. "Just in time—everybody else is here."

As Savannah reached the front door, Mrs. Fuller met her there in order to whisper in her ear before they got to the table. "There's only one woman in town pretty enough for *that* minister," she said.

"Shush," Savannah said. "Quite impossible."

"Oh, I already have it all worked out for you," she laughed. Mrs. Fuller was a true boardinghouse cook— cheerful, plump, a feminine mechanic with the pans, and a mysterious force of nature among the sauces.

Savannah washed up quickly and made her way back out to the dining room. The other boarders were already gathered, and Savannah looked at them with her usual mixture of affection and annoyance. She was working on that annoyance—it was not nearly what it had been several years ago. Sometimes it wasn't even there at all. Savannah was quick-witted, but just as quick with her tongue, and quick-tempered if she didn't watch it carefully. And it had been her misfortune to live in the same house with several boarders who were not nearly so quick, but who were unfortunately not aware of any notable discrepancies between themselves and others who were. But they were all dears, Savannah told herself again. She really was making headway.

Mrs. Fuller set the Sunday roast on the table, and sat down at the head of the table. Savannah sat to her right, and across from her was Bernie McDowell, an amateur theologian and fond critic of sermons. He was eager for Mrs. Fuller to say grace so that he could start in on Pastor Thomas's submission to the critics this very morning. To his left was a young man who worked at the feed store, Forrest Sampson, who was desperately in love with Miss Eleanor Simpson, straight across from him, who would only have to change one *letter* in her name, if only she would consent to be his wife, which was not going to happen any time soon if Forrest remained as tongue-tied as he had been up to the present.

To Miss Simpson's right was Jack Smith, who was as sturdy and predictable as his name might seem to indicate. He had lived in the boardinghouse for two years, ever since his wife had died; he owned and operated the hardware and dry goods store on Main Street. Mrs. Fuller was giving him an appropriate amount of time for grieving before she began making him aware of his clear and manifest need for a wife. Across from

Jack was Taylor Alfsson, a teller at the bank and a main source of information about Alan Lambeth's routine and characteristic rages there. Taylor would have known more about those rages first hand if Lambeth ever found out that his rollicking stories at the boardinghouse were the main but unspoken reason why Savannah had not even considered giving Lambeth the time of day.

Mrs. Warner, now in her nineties, no longer came to the table, but took her meals in her room. Mrs. Fuller was still able to care for her without too much trouble, but was beginning to wonder how long she would be able to do so. Savannah had gotten into the pattern of visiting Mrs. Warner several times a week in order to read to her for an hour or so.

At the opposite end of the table from Mrs. Fuller sat Elizabeth Sarandon, Savannah's rival for Alan Lambeth's affection. But of course there was no rivalry at all, for as far as Savannah was concerned Elizabeth could have him, and the sooner the better. However Elizabeth could not feel any depth of sincerity in this sentiment—and it was merely an unexpressed sentiment, for they had never talked about it—because she *thought* that Savannah was merely playing coy with Lambeth's affections, and she *knew* that Savannah was prettier than she was. That was enough to establish a settled enmity toward Savannah, although—with just a few exceptions—it had been consistently covered over with a sugar glaze, mingled strangely throughout with a grudging respect.

And Savannah *was* prettier, but it would have been much more of a contest if Elizabeth had been able to deal with a look of disdain that she perpetually had. Savannah, by contrast, was open and cheerful, and quick to laugh. Her hair, when she wasn't wearing it in her official schoolteacher bun, was a thick auburn waterfall down on her shoulders. She had a beautiful figure, and a slightly tip-tilted nose. Because she was quick to laugh, her teeth, which were straighter and whiter than Elizabeth thought they ought to have been, had been seen many times laughing around that very table. Elizabeth had been looking at Savannah again, and she made herself look down at her plate.

Mrs. Fuller finished saying her standard grace, and Bernie cleared his throat portentously. "Yes, Bernie," Mrs. Fuller said. "Was it something about the sermon?"

"Well, of course," Bernie replied. Bernie, an earnest little man in his late twenties, an odd mixture of toughness, insecurity, and conceit. He was slight of build, but he worked at the sawmill, and for the most part acquitted himself well there. He had come to believe, for various reasons, that he was destined for higher things, and his penchant for theology was one of the reasons why he considered himself an aspirant toward those higher things. He was scared of Savannah but, as he told himself, he was consistently careful in his speech around her, because his concern was to not lead her on. It wouldn't be fair, he told himself. Not gentlemanly.

"The sermon," Mrs. Fuller prompted.

"Yes," Bernie responded. "The sermon. Pastor Goforth seemed generally well-prepared this week—not at all like his first sermon—but I heard one thing that was a slight concern to me."

Savannah caught herself just in time. She found that she was about to defend last week's sermon, and to do so in spite of completely agreeing with Bernie about it. *That* was not a good sign. She found herself coloring slightly, and then she noticed that Mrs. Fuller had noticed it. Mrs. Fuller knew her very well, and was shrewder than most all of her friends. To prevent anyone *else* from noticing, she asked a question she ordinarily would not ask, which was, "What was the slight concern?"

"Well, Pastor Goforth comes to us from Princeton, so this shouldn't be a surprise, but there seemed to be more than a hint of infralapsarianism in his treatment of election. Didn't it seem that way to you?"

Reactions around the table were mixed, but everyone was cautiously polite. Savannah was the only one who had ever even encountered that word before, and she still didn't know what it meant. Forrest was busy thinking about Eleanor, Elizabeth was thinking about Savannah, and Jack, Eleanor, Taylor, Mrs. Fuller and Savannah were looking straight at Bernie, waiting for more.

Finally Jack said, "What difference does it make?"

This was the only invitation that Bernie needed, and so he began to talk, waving his fork languidly over his cooling potatoes. "It makes all the difference in the world . . ." he began. Theology was going to be his ticket out of the sawmill.

Savannah listened intently, interested in spite of herself, and finally blurted out, "You mean that God created the world so that He could have somebody to damn?"

"No, no," Bernie said. "That's what people always say, but it is a canard . . ."

At that moment, the little bell in Mrs. Warner's room rang, and Savannah nodded at Mrs. Fuller. "I'll get it," Savannah said. She was gone for a small while, taking Mrs. Warner her tea, and when she returned, and offered tea to the whole table, the subject had moved on. Actually, it is not quite accurate to say the subject had moved on. Taylor had started to make fun of Bernie, and Mrs. Fuller had then decreed that the topic was not a subject fit for the Sabbath anyway, which it wasn't.

Savannah sat back down to her cup of tea, and Mrs. Fuller said, "Did anyone smell the pies baking yesterday?" They all had, which is why no one had left the table, especially not Jack. Mrs. Fuller had less work before her than she was actually imagining.

"What kind?" Jack said hopefully. Mrs. Fuller was disappearing into the kitchen, and said "Apple" over her shoulder.

"Aside from your *infrasssp*, whatever that was, I do have some news about your new pastor." Taylor went to the Swedish Baptist church several blocks away from the Presbyterian church, and was not interested in the doctrinal issues that roiled the Presbyterians.

But he was interested in people, and how people responded to people.

"You should have heard Mr. Lambeth talking about your new Pastor Thomas this last Friday. Some people from your church were in his office—I think their name is Weston—and he left his door open—he does that on purpose, I think—and he was saying loudly that the sermon last Sunday was a disaster on wheels."

Savannah found herself reacting again, but this time she showed no sign of it. "Stay right where you are," she told herself sternly.

This time she was aware of her defensive reaction, and was able to restrain it more easily than when Bernie had brought up the tender subject. But she was still concerned. Mr. Lambeth was in more of a position to do harm to the church if he began agitating. Bernie was just a talker. Mr. Lambeth was not.

"I think that whatever happened last Sunday," Savannah said, "it is under control now. The sermon today was a fine specimen . . . of the sermonic arts."

"Sermonic arts?" Eleanor said.

"I couldn't think what to say. It was a fine sermon. I think Mr. Lambeth will have to look elsewhere if he wants to find fault."

Mrs. Fuller reappeared, and began placing pieces of pie before each of them.

"Oh, I think he fully intends to find fault," Taylor said. "If not the sermons, then something else. I was talking to Mr. Dooley once, the old-timer who lives down at the Hotel, and he told me about the time that

Wyatt Earp rode through, back in the day. The sheriff then was a retired gunfighter from down Utah way, and when those two met, you could hear the air just a crackling around them. It was a good thing they met at a church picnic, Dooley said. This reminds me of that. It seems that Mr. Lambeth knew right off that Pastor Thomas Goforth was not going to be his fishing companion for life."

Taylor had a shock of thick sandy red hair, and several constellations of freckles across the bridge of his nose. He had a quick and ready smile, and a bright wit. He didn't know it yet, but theology actually *was* going to be his ticket out of the bank. But for the present, he was happy with his work—Mr. Lambeth's tirades notwithstanding—and doing anything else had not yet occurred to him.

"Did Mr. Lambeth say anything else?" Savannah asked.

"No, no, just what a mess the sermon was. But he said that in twenty different ways. And there was a lot of cussing. Do all you Presbyterians talk like that?"

"No," said Mrs. Fuller, Bernie, and Savannah.

"I was just jibing," Taylor laughed. "Most of you are fine Christians. But I work for that man. He is a banker and a man of business, and so he has to join *some* church. How else can you meet people in such a way as to show them you are morally upright? But whatever church he wound up joining, the pastor of it would have his hands full—Mr. Lambeth is as fully heathen as the king of the Amalekites."

Savannah was poking at her pie with her fork. What was her duty to Pastor Thomas? She didn't want to pass on gossip. She didn't want him to not know if Lambeth was after him. But she didn't want to talk with Pastor Thomas about *anything* serious. And she didn't want to not talk with him either.

She tasted the pie, which was very good.

The old timers still called it Paradise City, or sometimes Paradise Valley. As the apostle Paul once noted on another subject, everyone was fully convinced in his own mind. But technically the unnamed person who registered the town with its first post office had just called it Paradise for short, and that was the name that had caught on. A few of the old timers objected, saying that it might be Paradise *now*, given that all the women were no longer back east, but the town was named earlier than that. But after the women began to arrive, the grumbling didn't exactly subside, although it did become a bit more good-natured. There had been one brief period when some people tried to call the town Hog Heaven—the camas root being plentiful, and a particular favorite with the pigs. But that name had failed to grip, and Paradise easily won out.

The farming was good in the surrounding fields, and off to the east the logging was just as good. But the thing that really put Paradise on the map was the decision of the state legislature to settle the masthead university of the state there in Paradise. This was an unusual move in that Paradise was way up north in the panhandle, but some thought that this was intended to make amends for the way that the state capital had been stolen—quite literally stolen—from Lewiston.

Lewiston, not far from Paradise, had been the capital of the territory, but when Lincoln was shot it had created a *lot* of turmoil, and an opportunity created by the distraction. In the immediate tumult after the assassination, a few civic-minded brigands had taken it upon themselves to make sure that the capital city was relocated down south in Boise. So they showed up in Lewiston with their guns, and commandeered the state seal, along with all the other official paraphernalia, and carted it off with them. It was as naked a power grab as you could ever hope to find in a history book about Vikings, but to their credit the Southerners had been kind of sheepish about it after the fact. Their sense of wrongdoing was not pronounced enough to make them want to undo the wrong, but it was enough to induce them to put the state university in Paradise as a consolation prize. That had happened in the waning years of the 19th century, and so it was then that the small town had really begun to flourish.

A minor gold rush around the same time had helped the local economy some, but there had not been enough gold on the mountain to keep the mines open whenever the price of gold went down, which it did from time to time, and so nothing really ever came of that.

The main roads in town were decent, or as good as macadamized roads could be. Main Street ran north and south, turned into highway at the edge of town, one which ran all the way up to Canada. This was a source of consternation to settlers from states like Nebraska, where Main Street was always supposed to run east-west, but they eventually got used to it. Many of the side streets were simply graveled, and some of them were still just dust and dirt. Most of the year they were passable, but when it began to rain in the late autumn, the mud was abundant and more than a little formidable. Third Street was the other main road, and it ran east and west. Going west you ran into Washington State within just a few miles, and going east you would run up a long sloping hill, pass East City Park on your left, and nothing past that but the edge of town, eight miles of prime farmland, and after that the wilderness, countless miles of pine trees.

There was an old decayed fort from the time of the last Indian wars that could still be made out, but most of the area north of the city park was just a very nice neighborhood now. As a token of respect for their past, they called it the Fort Russell area, but nobody really noticed the outlines of the abandoned fort. But despite the nice homes, touches of the rustic were still very much in evidence. The wealthier citizens of Paradise lived up there on that modest hill, but they still, many of them, kept a cow. A boy would come around every morning, gather up the various cows, and walk them all out to a pasture on the edge of town. In the evening, he would walk them all back in again, the residents would get their fresh milk in the morning, and the whole operation would be repeated again.

Cars were just starting to make a serious appearance, and it was expected by everyone that in just a few years there would be many more. But for now, there were still many on horseback, and not a few horsedrawn wagons. For those who traveled on foot, it was possible to walk from the east side of town, where the cows were pasturing, over to the west side, just beyond downtown, in about twenty minutes.

On the south end of Main Street, construction had begun on a new fire station for the volunteer fire department. That new building was to be of brick, and the old clapboard station was looking forward to its coming retirement.

The wealthier homes in town were decorated in the ways most homes back East were done in that day—a heavy emphasis on dark and heavy wallpaper, drapes with fringe, lampshades with fringe, and brass and mahogany in abundance. Some, trying to vie with the silver barons up north laid it on thick. Other more sensible people showed some restraint, but everyone was working with the same basic materials. Furnishings were mostly thick and substantial.

The weather was generally mild, although Paradise *was* capable of having a real winter. That would happen every five years or so. But most winters brought snow, and then rain, and then snow, and snow a bit more, and then melt again. Below-zero temperatures for a week or two were common, and in the summer the same thing in the opposite direction usually brought temperatures over a hundred. But for the most part, once spring decided to arrive and remain settled, the weather was steadily glorious through October.

That Sunday evening, the day of Pastor Goforth's second sermon, having been just such a glorious day, Savannah stood on the porch of Mrs. Fuller's boardinghouse, arms crossed contentedly, watching the sun go down. She had not yet gotten used to how gaudy the sunsets could be here, showing no self-restraint at all. When she had had enough—although she would never really have enough—she sighed and turned to go inside the house.

THE POTATO
SALAD INCIDENT

BELLONA, the goddess of war, daughter of
Phorcys and Ceto.
ANTHON, *A CLASSICAL DICTIONARY*

Elizabeth Sarandon had long admired Savannah and was perpetually annoyed by her. The principle reason she was annoyed by her is that she found herself compulsively imitating Savannah, and this put her out of countenance with herself. She regularly annoyed *herself* when she was around Savannah, and this made her annoyed with Savannah. It didn't help that Savannah never seemed to notice.

If Savannah subscribed to a magazine, Elizabeth found herself wanting to. She was bright enough not to let this impulse show to others, but she could not keep it from being apparent to herself. And she hated that in herself. She had an acute, artistic eye—a number of her drawings up in her room could attest to that—and this was part of the problem. She couldn't help noticing things; she couldn't stop *seeing*.

One time Savannah had purchased a handbag at the department store where Elizabeth worked, and it was all Elizabeth could do to prevent herself from buying the one remaining matching handbag. She fought with herself for two days over that, and then gave in. She bought the bag, smuggled it back to her room, and that evening made a catty comment to Savannah wondering why she felt the need to buy the same kind of bag that Elizabeth had.

But Savannah just laughed, easily, and offered to pull hers from public circulation. "That way nobody will think I am copying you," she said.

And there was the problem. It was ludicrous to think that anybody would ever think that Savannah was copying anybody. She was at ease with herself, and did not appear to be looking out the corner of her eye at anybody. Elizabeth simultaneously envied that freedom, and could not comprehend it.

Another time Elizabeth and Savannah had quarreled in the kitchen. That is, Elizabeth had quarreled until Savannah noticed, and then Savannah immediately dropped it. Elizabeth couldn't even remember what that had been about now. But she did remember, and remember vividly, how Savannah had look startled, had bitten her tongue before she said *oh*, and then deferred to Elizabeth immediately.

Elizabeth was always aware of where Savannah was, what she was doing, what she was wearing. The slights that inevitably resulted were taken by Elizabeth as clear indications of an air of superiority and barely hidden animus—but the more obvious it was that Savannah was not thinking about Elizabeth at all, which became clear regularly, the more that was taken as indications of additional malice. But Savannah was very rarely aware of what Elizabeth was doing. She loved her, as a neighbor and as the Good Book instructs, but she did not study her. And *that* was a mortal offense.

A picnic dedicated to welcoming the new pastor was organized within the first month of Thomas's arrival. Mrs. Fuller was the first instigator, but some of the other ladies who were less busy than she was were happy to take it from her. The picnic was on a Sunday afternoon at East City Park, just a few blocks from the church. Most of the families were going to pack their lunches and bring them along to church, a handful in cars, and the others in their wagons.

Paradise had many months of very fine weather, but September was always a contender for the finest among them. February was never even considered as a prospect. Savannah smiled at that thought, closed the door behind her, and started to head off for church with her picnic basket over her arm. She got out to the street, and suddenly started. "Such a ninnyhammer!" She then went back to Mrs. Fuller's car, and put her basket in the back seat. Mrs. Fuller usually walked to church also, following Savannah by about fifteen minutes, but she had distinctly mentioned that she was going to be taking the car today. And there was nothing in Savannah's basket that needed to be kept cool.

The swelter of August was gone, and the slightest touch of autumn was in the back of her throat. Nevertheless, the sun shone in a way that promised a good friendship for the rest of the day. Savannah promised her friendship in return, and set out confidently. She wondered what Pastor Thomas was going to preach on today. Her thoughts drifted toward him easily. After a few moments, she caught herself. *Too* easily. *Impossible,* she thought, and shook herself. *Already too tragic,* she thought again.

Thomas was outside the church, greeting his parishioners as they started to gather to the church. Savannah found her pulse quickening, and rebuked herself savagely. He was a very nice man, a nice pastor. Not *possible.* She forced her recalcitrant thoughts into a back room, swallowed bravely, and walked past him. "Good morning, pastor," she said, a little archly, and sailed into the church.

The service was good. The message was well done, as usual, and the singing seemed better than usual. Attendance was up. When the final benediction was pronounced, Savannah found Mrs. Fuller and walked with her to the car. "I feel silly driving such a short distance," she said.

"But if you do it, I won't feel silly riding with you," Savannah laughed. "And I can help you explain and apologize to people."

"Shush," Mrs. Fuller said.

Perhaps the singing had been better in church today because more people came, or had made a point of coming. If there was going to be a picnic right afterward, even some of the outlying farmers would be more willing to make a point of coming in for something like that.

But Savannah's heart dropped when she saw Alan Lambeth making his way across the grass, carrying his small basket. He had not renewed his attempts at courtship since last year, when Savannah had finally communicated her complete lack of interest. In the three very difficult conversations, each one of which Savannah felt was abundantly clear, she had felt nothing but awkward. But nothing had been abundantly clear to Lambeth until that third and final conversation. When it had finally settled in on him that the poor schoolteacher wanted nothing to do with the rich banker, and never had wanted anything to do with him, which was a kind of thinking he had never seen up close before, he had taken it ill. He had left in a cloud of indignation, very stiff and very proper.

Since that time, he had gone out of his way to be cordial and warm and *very* brief in all his interactions with Savannah. He was above it all and did not care,

and he carried it all in a way that displayed to insightful people the fact that he cared very much. He never
saw her without greeting her, and Savannah always
felt that a quarter of an inch beneath his warm greeting was a layer of ice that approached glacial thick-
nesses. And here he was, coming across the park in
her direction.

Fortunately, he picked a spot on the other side of
the growing gathering, spread out his blanket, and
then stooped over his basket to work at something for
a moment. In spite of herself, Savannah found herself
trying to figure out what he could be doing. It did not
look as though he was settling in. After a moment, he
stood up again with a small bowl in his hand, and he
started to walk straight toward her. *No, please, no,* Savannah found herself muttering, and discovered that
her muttering had no effect on his approach at all.

When he arrived, he bowed slightly, and said,
"Miss Westmoreland, I wonder if you would do me
the honor of trying my grandmother's recipe for potato salad. I am told it is quite good. I would value your
good opinion."

That last sentence had enough ironic emphasis to be
fully understood by her in two ways, but not so much
that any bystander who overheard would do anything
but take it at face value. *I would value your good opinion*
meant that he knew that a good opinion of him to be an
impossibility, the potato salad standing in for him as a
metaphor, and so this is why it was said in such a way as
to indicate that he was serenely above it all. He did not

care in the slightest, which is why he had been planning this moment since the picnic was first announced.

At the same time Savannah was mortified to notice—not knowing why she was mortified—that Pastor Thomas had come up on her left. There was no reason that he shouldn't come up to them, but Savannah still felt that he ought to have been more considerate. She flushed, but very slightly. Savannah's eyes opened a bit wider, and quietly she thanked God that she was able to speak.

"Mr. Lambeth," she said, grateful that every word was true and she did not have to face the temptation to fib. "I am very sorry, but potato salad simply does not agree with me. I do not know why, or how, but I have not been able to have any for many years now. I am very sorry about it, because I loved potato salad as a girl. But I get a rash on my forearms. I am sure your grandmother's recipe would be quite lovely." And she smiled graciously and handed the bowl back to him.

More words would have been exchanged, but some organizing noises were coming from the other side of the crowd. Lambeth suddenly disappeared. It seemed as though most of the congregation had assembled, had their blankets spread out, and their picnic baskets situated, and so Mr. Felton clapped his hands and got everyone's attention. Mr. Felton was the stated clerk for the session of elders, and had already become fast friends with Thomas.

"Normally," he said, "we would ask our good pastor to say the blessing, but since this here event is

welcoming and honoring *his* arrival, we will all take
the risk of me saying the blessing instead. I still think
we can get the job done."

Everybody laughed, and when it was quiet Mr.
Felton said grace, and everybody turned with a will
to their baskets. Things were quiet for a few minutes
as the congregation of saints bent to their happy work.

Savannah was sitting with Mrs. Fuller, the third oc-
cupant of their blanket being Jack Smith, ensnared by
the prospect of the pies he had seen cooling on the sill
yesterday. Pastor Thomas was two blankets over, sitting contentedly with the Feltons, his tall frame somehow managing to sit comfortably on the ground.

The second time Alan Lambeth approached her,
she did not see him coming. He suddenly appeared
right in front of them again, the offending bowl of
potato salad in his hand again, and something of an
apologetic expression on his face. "I am sorry to intrude again," he said with excessive politeness, "but it
occurred to me that you might have had the same kind
of reaction to this that my sister once had. She was also
unable to have potato salad when we were children,
but after we were grown, she tried it once, and had no
reaction at all. And so I was wondering if you would
be willing to try it on a venture."

The issue between the two combatants was by this
point simply a contest of wills. Lambeth had no sister, and he hoped that Savannah would be gullible to
take him up on the invitation, and he wished the rash
of all rashes upon her. All that mattered was that he

somehow prevail in what had become, inexplicably to him, a showdown.

Savannah was not as warm as she had been on the first refusal, but she was still perfectly cordial. "I am afraid that I can't afford to risk it. The delights of the potato salad would only be for a Sunday afternoon, however delightful it might be, and the rash, at least when I was a girl, would last for a week and a half." She handed the bowl back to him a second time, with equal decisiveness. Perhaps with an emphasized decisiveness. He bowed his head slightly, saying nothing, and made his way off again.

The picnic continued on, a delightful and delighting event. Savannah enjoyed the next hour visiting with friends, all of whom came by to speak with her. Some were moving around the picnic, stopping at various blankets as though they were making social calls on various houses. Others remained with their blankets in order to receive visitors. The trees were still leafy green and towered over them all, providing just the right amount of shade. It was altogether a most pleasant afternoon.

When Savannah was done chatting with Helen, a friend who lived out in the county and who did not get into town as often as she would like, she turned around and jumped, startled. In spite of herself, she gasped. There, standing right behind her, was Lambeth again, holding what was by now an innocent bowl of potato salad that had somehow managed to become an outrage. Savannah looked at him fiercely and said nothing. He had come up intending just to leave the bowl on top of her picnic basket and then simply walk away. He could exult in the moral victory later. But she turned around at just the wrong moment. Their eyes met, and the wounded animus that had formed in him when she had definitively rejected him the year before swelled up in him. He found he could no more control it than a geyser could control the next eruption. He leaned forward, and between clenched teeth, whispered several fierce obscenities at her—but despite his anger, he took care (or so he thought) that no one else could hear him. He put the potato salad down on the lid of her picnic basket, dug a hole in the turf with the heel of his boot as he swiveled around to go, and strode off.

The first two times he had tried to deliver the potato salad, Savannah had borne his overdone courtesies with equanimity. She had been courteous, friendly, and distant. Her behavior had been fully consistent with her membership vows in the church and she knew it. She had diligently pursued the church's purity and peace. But now . . . she stooped and picked up the bowl.

And yet here, with his vile words still ringing in her ear and with the bowl of potato salad in her hand for the third time, she was momentarily seized with a paralyzing fury. Alan Lambeth continued to slowly walk off. Savannah was in the grip of an emotion she had never felt before.

Mrs. Fuller looked at her with alarm. It seemed to her like that moment when a toddler crashes in the next room, and nothing follows but an eerie silence. Experienced parents know that the child is busy gathering up all the available oxygen in the room, and a wail of wails may be expected presently. Mrs. Fuller wasn't expecting a wail, but the situation was similarly charged, and equally ominous. "Now Savannah . . ."

But Savannah wasn't listening. She was deaf to the world and its cares. She drew herself up to her full height, and hurled the bowl of potato salad at the back of Lambeth's head.

Many years before, her father had spent a considerable amount of time teaching her how to throw—much to her mother's dismayed concerns about the threat to ladylikeness—and Savannah, as her mother had feared, had proved to be an apt student. So even after these years, her aim was still true, and she threw like someone who knew how to throw. The bowl sailed in a straight line, as if an arrow shot from a bow, but the bowl slowly turned over, rotating in flight. It grazed the top of Lambeth's head, but because it was upside down by the time it reached him, it knocked his hat off and deposited half its contents on the top of his head.

Those who saw the whole thing unfold—about ten people—gasped. Actually most of them gasped. Two of them laughed, one of those being Pastor Thomas. But he caught himself immediately and resumed a look of solemn pastoral concern. Lambeth wheeled around, glared, brushed the potato salad out of his hair, took a step toward Savannah, thought better of it, looked around for his hat, snatched it up furiously, and then picked up the bowl and strode off. Savannah had returned his glare steadily.

Pastor Thomas walked toward Savannah, but a little uncertainly. There had been nothing in seminary about this kind of thing at *all*. She was plainly a firecracker, a pippin, a beautiful volcano. She turned around, and saw Pastor Thomas approaching her. She exploded at him with some controlled ferocity. "Well, I *do* understand why the pastor would come around with a look of concern. You simply *must* have a Scripture passage for me." She then caught herself. She had had a number of things that she was brimming to tell Alan Lambeth, but because he had deserted the field of battle, all her music was bottled up within her. It wouldn't be fair to direct any of that toward Pastor Thomas. She bit her lip but was still very angry. She had to be fair.

"I plainly need to go speak to him," Pastor Thomas said. "*What* did he say to you?"

Mrs. Fuller could tell that Savannah was near tears, but knew that if *that* happened they would only be hot tears, angry tears. "It's complicated, pastor," Mrs. Fuller said. "I will come by the parsonage tomorrow and explain it to you. There's a history," she added.

Pastor Thomas nodded, dubiously. He was not sure that he could hear anything that would account for any of this. Savannah had turned abruptly away and was busy packing her basket, and then glanced over at Mrs. Fuller. "I can walk home," she said. "You only brought the car because you were going to go see your cousin afterward." Mrs. Fuller arched her eyebrows as much as to ask about where Lambeth had gone. Savannah knew her pretty well, and simply said, *"He* went north."

"Well, then," Pastor Thomas said.

The next day, Mrs. Fuller did not come to explain anything to Thomas because Savannah wouldn't let her. By Sunday evening, Savannah had calmed down considerably, and by the time she went to bed, she was philosophical. "I will go instead," she said firmly. "There is something else I need to tell him, and this is as good a time as any. In fact, perhaps better."

And that is how it came about that Savannah was standing on the sidewalk outside the parsonage. It was an attractive, small house, and the study where the pastor would meet with parishioners was on the side of the house, with a separate walk that went up to an outside door. Savannah had been there many times before, but this was the first time since Pastor Eugene had died.

She swallowed hard, twice, and then tapped on the door, twice. To her surprise, Mr. Felton answered the door and opened it wide. "Come in, come in," he said cheerfully. He turned and spoke to Pastor Thomas inside. "Miss Savannah to see you," he said. He turned back to her, nodded his head slightly, and said, "I was just on my way."

"Please," Savannah said hurriedly. "Please, could you stay for a moment? You are on the session also."

"I have a few moments," Mr. Felton said, looking at his watch.

They both walked back into the study. Pastor Thomas had been sitting behind his desk, and he stood up as they walked in. There were two armchairs on the Persian carpet in front of his desk, and he gestured warmly, inviting them to sit. Mr. Felton didn't need the invitation, because the far chair was the one he had just left when he went to answer the door. Savannah had gasped inwardly when she came in—the study was teeming with books. She had not seen so many books since she had come West. Pastor Eugene had books, but nothing like this.

"Sit down, sit down," Pastor Thomas was saying.

When they were all seated, and the pleasantries were done, Savannah cleared her throat and said, "I assume you know the general topic of my visit?" Both men nodded.

"I have three things I needed to tell you, and the fact that Mr. Felton is here makes it simpler. At least two of them should concern the session of elders."

"Go on," said Pastor Thomas, interested at the way she was beginning. He knew the topic of her visit, but was surprised at the approach she appeared to be taking.

She cleared her throat again. "First, Pastor Thomas, please let me seek your forgiveness for snapping at you yesterday. I was very angry, but not at you, and I should not have spoken that way. About you having a Scripture passage for me, I mean."

"Your apology is accepted," Pastor Thomas said. "And thank you."

"After that, there are three other things," she said again. "The first is that I wanted you to know that if I needed to seek forgiveness from Mr. Lambeth, I would be most willing to do it. But I wanted you to hear the two other things I have to say first, and then ask you to give me your advice as to whether I needed to seek forgiveness. If you will let me speak to those two things first, I will be most willing to follow your counsel, whatever it is."

Pastor Thomas nodded again.

"The second is I have an acquaintance who works at the bank. He informs me—and I believe the information is reliable—that Mr. Lambeth is trying to foment unhappiness with your performance as a pastor."

At this Thomas and Mr. Felton exchanged glances. That was actually what they had been talking about before Savannah came in. People like Lambeth don't foment trouble with half measures. The two men sat silently while Savannah summarized what Taylor had told them all. She had gotten Taylor's permission first and had carefully left his name out of it.

"I know that there is not enough here to condemn anyone, because there are not two witnesses, but I do believe that there is enough here to ask you to walk carefully."

Thomas and Mr. Felton both nodded. Savannah did not have two witnesses to this behavior of Lambeth's, but unknown to her, *they* now did. The Westons had not appreciated Lambeth's harangue as much as Lambeth had thought they might, and had already talked to Mr. Felton about it.

"The last thing is this. If Mr. Lambeth had just been a boor with the potato salad, I trust that my manners would have been up to the challenge. I do not believe that I have a right to throw something at one of your parishioner's heads just because he was being tedious. The third time he came back with the potato salad, he leaned over and said something to me, and I believed I had to do something. I was angry when I did it, but I do not believe that it was unrighteous. And I did not let the sun go down on it."

"What did he say?" Mr. Felton asked.

"You have raised a point of some delicacy," Savannah said. "And I thought you would ask that, and I knew I wouldn't want to say it to you. I took the liberty of writing it down for you before I came."

With that, she handed a small piece of folded paper across the desk to Pastor Thomas. She had previously thought through how she could possibly do this, and had worked out in her mind the importance of not seeming like a prim schoolmarm, but still doing the right thing. She mostly succeeded. Pastor Thomas opened and read it, and his eyes got wide. "He said *this*?"

Savannah nodded.

"A hundred years ago, duels would have been fought over this," Thomas said. "Maybe wars."

He silently handed the paper across to Mr. Felton, who first whistled, then pursed his lips and said nothing. Thomas sat quietly for a moment. "Did anyone else hear him?" he asked.

Savannah nodded. "Yes. Mrs. Fuller did. He wasn't as quiet as he thought he was being."

"Well, the immediate question is an easy one," Pastor Thomas said. "Given this, your apologizing to him is out of the question. I have had several people ask me about the incident, wondering if I am going to *do* anything, and I now have something to tell them. I will say that an apology is in fact necessary, and I am going to try to secure one for the peace of the congregation. But it will not be an apology rendered to Mr. Lambeth but rather one—if it happens—coming *from* Mr. Lambeth."

"Thank you," Savannah said. They all sat quietly for a moment, and then Savannah got up suddenly. "Well, I do have things to do. I must be going on. Thank you for your time." And with that, she seemed to glide from the room, like a ship under sail.

The two men had stood when she stood, and when they heard the door close, they both sat down again. Mr. Felton sat slumped in his chair, with his fingers splayed together, and as he looked over at Thomas, he laughed out loud.

"What?" said Pastor Thomas, self-consciously.

"My boy—and though you are my pastor, on this subject I will insist upon calling you *my dear boy*—you are in deep trouble."

"With Lambeth? I can handle Lambeth."

Mr. Felton snorted. "No, not Lambeth. I have high hopes for you with Lambeth. With that young lady what just exited the premises."

Thomas rubbed his face with both hands. "I take your point." He wished he could tell Mr. Felton all that was on his mind—he had only known him a matter of weeks, but already trusted him fully. He could at least tell him *some* of it. "I take your meaning," he continued. "Or at least I think I do. A gentle and quiet spirit, truly such as Peter describeth—a real Christian. As well as a spitfire and a beautiful hellcat, as per Paul in Titus 2."

"You noticed then?"

"It was hard to miss. Unlike Mr. Lambeth's head, which *should* have been hard to miss, but wasn't. I have not seen a truer arm in years. The way she stepped into it . . . her follow through . . . that woman is a high-hearted marvel."

"There is something else to all this, as well," Mr. Felton said.

"And what is that?"

"The expectations of the congregation. What percentage of the congregation might you think already has you two paired off? And is wondering what is taking you so long?"

"All of the married women?"

Mr. Felton smiled grimly. "Let us assume that as a minimum. Now—assuming as I do that you are not entirely opposed to the prospect—you do need to be careful. If you do anything to get tongues wagging before the time, some well-meaning soul is going to start giving *her* helpful advice. Or worse yet, will start pressuring her. And one thing I think can be safely assumed about Savannah Westmoreland: she would not respond well to pressure. Especially if someone were to slyly hint to her that you were somehow behind the pressure."

"You are right about all of that, including the fact that I am not entirely opposed to the prospect. And the word *entirely* there is entirely ironic."

"So you are interested in her then?"

Pastor Thomas glanced sharply at Mr. Felton. "It is far more complicated than that. At some point I am sure—when I know more—that I will want to talk with you about it. But as it is, my sentiments alternate between thinking on some days that it is inevitable and on others that it is impossible. These are not reconcilable. You can't split the difference."

"No," Mr. Felton said. "You can't."

THE CATCH

Stay me with flagons, comfort me with apples:
For I am sick of love.
SONG OF SONGS 2:5

Savannah had won the admiration of Sheriff Barnes a little over a year after she had arrived in Paradise. Of course, he had known who she was—for everyone who had his hair cut in the town's one barbershop knew *that*—but he didn't think anything more about it than that. He just knew that there was a "pretty lady" teaching high school now.

One day in the late fall, Savannah had worked a little late at the school, and was walking home in the late afternoon darkness. Two rowdies who worked at the mill had gotten paid earlier that day, and had come into town to celebrate. Although it was only 4:30 p.m., they had gotten an early start, and were already well-oiled.

The sheriff had considered it part of his responsibility to remain apprised of just such potentialities, and as he had seen them both stagger into *The Silver Stirrup*, and as they had been making the kind of noise that indicated that there might be more exuberance to follow, he had walked past the saloon every fifteen minutes or so, just across the street. It was now about an hour later, and he stopped for a moment. There were sounds within that indicated they were about to emerge. Just then some motion caught his eye off to the left, and so Sheriff Barnes glanced up the street, toward the high school. With some alarm, he saw that Savannah was walking steadily down the sidewalk. Dusk was well advanced and the only reason he could see her was the light color of her dress, flashing as she walked.

He looked back at the bar, and at that moment the two men staggered out, whooping indiscriminately. They turned this way and that, righted themselves, and turned again, just in time to find themselves face-to-face with Savannah, blocking her way past them on the sidewalk. A deep puddle was in the gutter next to the sidewalk, preventing Savannah from stepping around them.

"Well, sweetheart!" one of them roared. "Thanks for meeting us here!" The other man roared with laughter at this profound witticism.

"Pardon me," Savannah said. "I would like to get past . . ."

"Where's your little sister?" the wit continued. "My friend here is lonesome." His friend laughed again. "Yeah, lonesome," he said. "I thought you were going to bring your little sister."

Savannah took a step back, but not in a way that was acting like she was anxious, not acting in any way concerned. She looked like she just wanted a little more room. Sheriff Barnes had decided that things had already gone a little bit farther than was healthy, and so he was halfway across the street by this point. In the dusk, no one noticed him, not Savannah, and not the men.

"Do you want to go dancing with us, darlin'?" the spokesman for the two said.

"No, thank you," she said. "But I would like to get past."

The sheriff came up on them, and appeared suddenly to their left. "Evening, gents," he said. "I think it is past time that you made yourselves scarce. Think you can make your way back to your rooms?"

The two men looked over to their left, startled. They had both spent the night in the sheriff's rooms on previous occasions, and instantly remembered how uncomfortable they were. "Uh, yes. Yes, we can make it home," the first man said.

"And I think you would be ill-advised to stop at any more . . . establishments . . . on your way there. If you go home and go to sleep now, you can end everything

on a celebratory note. If you keep on, as your mother used to say when you were rough-housing as kids,
somebody is going to get hurt."

Both of them looked at the sheriff, nodded slightly,
and stepped toward the building, and single file they
walked past Savannah. Without any further words,
they disappeared into the gloaming.

"Thank you, Sheriff . . .?"

"Barnes. My name is Barnes."

"My name is Savannah Westmoreland. Thank you
for intervening on my behalf. I appreciate it very much."

"You are most welcome." The sheriff nodded.
"But I must say that you didn't seem nearly as anxious as some women as I could mention might have
been. Are you a woman of high courage, or are you
just brave?"

"Or perhaps reckless?"

"Well, I didn't want to include that, being as we've
just now met."

Savannah had been holding her handbag in front
of her, and she now moved it. When she did, the sheriff
suddenly noticed that her right hand was in a curious
position behind her handbag. She moved the handbag
to the left, and held up a small derringer between her
thumb and forefinger.

"It is not a huge insurance policy. But it is a *sufficient* insurance policy," Savannah said.

At this the sheriff laughed out loud, tipped his hat
to her in the old fashion, and made his way down the
street, following the two men to make sure they had

done what they were instructed to do. When he was about fifty feet away, he started chuckling.

In the months to follow, he meditated on her calmness more than once. He decided that he would count himself as an admirer, and rejoiced that the hooligans at the high school—who accounted for a good third of his activities as sheriff—had someone on the premises who could take them in hand. Someone like *that* woman might be able to turn them into citizens.

It was the next Sunday evening, a week after the picnic, that Savannah realized, with some annoyance, that Pastor Thomas knew how to sing. The annoyance was mixed with gratitude and admiration, but when she first noticed that something involving that whole subject was churning within herself, which all happened quite quickly, the annoyance was winning.

This congregation of Presbyterian saints was a sturdy bunch, with the ways of the old West still within living memory, so if you kept them to the familiar and established hymns that they had learned from their mothers, they were fairly content and somewhat competent. But they had no notions beyond the rudiments of roaring the melody—the other lines of music in the hymnal they just assumed to be footings and pylons for the higher notes. Musicians fooled around with things like those. Nobody was supposed to *sing* them.

This had actually been the only thing that had dismayed Savannah about Paradise. She had a beautiful contralto voice, and had been a very able pianist when she was younger. She had attempted to organize a choir for the church a couple of times, but if a successful choir had been a great wide river, both her attempts had beached on sand bars, treacherous and unforeseen. Not only so, but the sand bars were pretty close to her side of the river.

The first time out, the problem had been the humility of those who were fairly decent at singing, but who knew they weren't all *that* good. Certainly not good enough for a choir, so very few people turned out. The second time the problem had been the non-humility of some who couldn't carry a tune in a peach basket, but who were unaware of this salient and fairly relevant point. Both times Savannah had given up after three practices.

But the occasion of her annoyance now was an impromptu social gathering on a Sunday evening after service at the home of her friend and (only) fellow musician, Sally Parker. On a whim, Sally had invited a number of parishioners to come over, and about twelve of them—single, mostly, and some young married couples without children—were able to do so. Pastor Thomas had been invited at the last moment, and because he saw Savannah was going to be there, he had been glad to join them. Sally had made several apple pies the day before and was delighted to be able to offer something to "company." So the group sat around visiting on her front porch for an hour or so, and there was a lot of laughter and storytelling. Pastor Thomas didn't say much, sitting in the corner of the porch, but he was obviously enjoying himself.

Savannah told a number of the stories, but her conscience was warning her not to be so forward, not to be so talkative. She was aware that she was more or less out there, carrying the conversation. That annoyed her in the first instance.

When it began to look as though the party was going to break up soon, Sally invited them all to conclude with several hymns. She had a piano which she invited Savannah to play, and she eagerly distributed some hymnals that she kept around for just such occasions. Savannah was used to that piano because Sally would invite her over regularly to let her keep up with her technique some.

So Savannah was seated at the piano, and was halfway through the first verse when she noticed that a strong male voice had decided to take up the bass line. "Friends may fail me, foes assail me . . . " Who could that be? When the song was over, she looked over her left shoulder and saw that it was Pastor Thomas.

"Well," she said tartly, "had I known we had a *musician* among us . . . " It then occurred to her that there was no way for this line to turn into a witticism by the end, so she stopped mid-sentence. That made the effect of her comment even more tart than it had been at the beginning, and she started kicking herself inside. Thomas only grinned.

"One more hymn," Sally said hurriedly. *Why did she do that?* Sally wondered. *Why did I do that?* Savannah wondered. She was annoyed that she had let her annoyance show, and she was also annoyed by his

singing, and she was annoyed with herself for being
so petty. Why shouldn't he know how to sing? If she
didn't like it when men didn't sing, why would she
be so annoyed if one of them did? What was wrong
with her?

After one more hymn, the party broke up, chattering happily. As it happened, largely because of
Thomas's smart and keen-eyed maneuvers going out
the front door, he managed to reach the front sidewalk at the same time that Savannah did. The other
guests were already down the sidewalk in either direction. "It is late," Thomas observed. "May I walk
you home?"

Savannah hoped that he couldn't hear her pulse.
She could certainly hear it. She didn't want him to walk
her home, she wanted him to walk her home in the
worst way, and she teetered back and forth in her soul.
After a long second, she thought of her rude comment
earlier, thought she needed to make up for it, and said,
"Thank you." Thomas moved easily to the street side
of the sidewalk, but thankfully did not present his arm
to her. His manners were impeccable.

They walked silently south toward Third Street,
alongside the park where they had been a week earlier. The silence continued until it became awkward and
uncomfortable, but then it extended some moments
beyond that until Savannah felt as if he were being quiet deliberately. So then it became comfortable again.

After several blocks, they would turn right and
walk down the long sloping hill, past the church,

toward downtown, where the boardinghouse was. The silence continued to be comfortable enough, but Savannah didn't know if that was because the silence was comfortable, or because she was terrified of him saying anything.

"You play the piano beautifully," he finally said.

"Thank you," she said.

His follow up statement was equal parts personal and pastoral and professional, but in different ways. "How is it that you don't play for the church more?" The woman who *did* play for the church, Mrs. Addie Bradshaw, was nowhere near as adept as Savannah had been that night, and as far as anyone could tell, had only one speed, which was moderately slow.

Savannah appreciated the diplomacy in the question, and knew that this was something he actually needed to know as the pastor. She was also delighted to be talking about a subject like music in the church, and not about another subject that might set her emotions to rioting in the streets.

"The position was already filled when I arrived," she said. "Addie is a dear soul, and asks me to play for her whenever she and her husband are visiting their people up north of Spokane. So I play three or four times a year. That is more than enough for me. Sally lets me practice at her piano often, so I have all the music that I need."

Pastor Thomas said something like "I see," and they walked on a little further. As they walked, Savannah noticed how much he simply *filled* the space next to her. She thought of his singing again, and wondered to herself again why she had made that comment, and then surprised herself by instantly coming up with an answer to that puzzle. She didn't like the answer very much.

Her previous pastor had known something about Savannah that no one else did. One of the central spiritual disciplines that Savannah had set for herself was the discipline of personal and transparent honesty, honesty to herself. She resisted a spirit of morbid introspection, but she had also resolved to be ruthless with herself. And that is how, as the result of long practice, she knew in an instant that she wanted to be with Thomas because he could lead her, and she also wanted Thomas gone and out of her life because . . . he would lead her. And she knew instantly that even if a relationship with him had been possible, which it fortunately was *not*, there was at least a part of her that would *still* want him far away.

There was no question but that Savannah was a shining star in the firmament of their small church community. She was gregarious, friendly, winsome, talented, and beautiful, and she had many dear friends. And she did get, she admitted to herself, a good bit of . . . no, it was not flattering attention . . . but it was attention that flattered. She never let it go to her head, but it would be fair to say she was not entirely unaffected by it either. And now, here was this man, filling up the space next to her. With him there, she would not be as central to . . . she would not be as noticed . . . no, it was *appalling* for her to think about herself in those terms.

So she knew that impulse was there, and she knew that she had that within her, and she detested it within her. But it seemed that this impulse was something that drove her to say things even before the attitude had made a formal entry into her conscious mind. But it had now, and it was pretty apparent to her that she wanted someone very much like Thomas appeared to be, and that another part of her didn't want anything of the kind.

But besides, marriage to a godly minister like Thomas was simply impossible. Just impossible. Her mind turned naturally, instinctively, instantly, to her time in Milwaukee. He could not fill that space for her. But with him *not* there, how was she going to learn what deference and surrender meant? How would she pursue this valuable spiritual lesson?

It was a moot point, anyway, because he couldn't ever be with her. But how was she to mortify the sin of wanting to be the one who dazzled? Was she upset with his singing because it distracted from her playing? When Savannah was being severe with herself this way, she sometimes went farther than she needed to in her self-recrimination, but she rarely made things up out of whole cloth. There was *something* there.

She was suddenly seized with an impulse to apologize for her comment while they were all singing, but she knew (at the same instant) that her comment didn't exactly require an apology, and that to do it she would have to open up far more than she could afford to open up. She couldn't explain anything without explaining everything, and so she decided to simply try to mend things, if anything needed mending, by simply being pleasant. Then she started rethinking that. She *would* be pleasant regardless. Pastor Thomas seemed to have ignored the whole thing anyway. He was walking her home, for pity's sake.

They were nearing her boardinghouse. By this point, Savannah had resolved how she would handle it, what she would do. She had practiced her speech in her head several times, hoping that Thomas would not resume conversation while she was rehearsing. When they got to the walk that led up to the house, she turned and spoke to him, warm, friendly, and distant. She was most courteous, but she was also seeking to communicate that this would go no further. It was a manner she had had to practice with men before.

"Thank you for walking me home," she said. "I am most grateful." She was disconcerted when she saw that Thomas had taken her meaning, but had simply grinned. She had meant to put him off, discouraging him, or she *thought* she had meant to. It worked other times. Perhaps she was sabotaging her own efforts. Perhaps there was a traitor in the ranks. He probably saw that she didn't mean it.

"Well," he said, "I suppose we will see one another again on Friday?"

"Friday?" she said, puzzled. "I am afraid I will be out of town on Friday . . ."

"That's what I mean. The mayor invited me to come to the event at the Davenport in Spokane. He said that he had invited you also, and that you were coming."

The mayor was constantly a booster of all things Paradise, and loved to take excursions to nearby big events with representative notables from his small but nevertheless *yearning* town. He was always at it, and usually rotated the names of those invited. This was the first time he had invited Pastor Thomas, and the third time he had invited Savannah. The Davenport had just recently been built with a flood of new money from the silver mines up north, and this was an important event for all the regional towns. Gov. Hart of Washington was going to be there.

"Oh," Savannah said. "I didn't know that." She didn't let her flustered spirits show. After a moment, she added, "You will be most welcome, of course."

"I would hope so," Thomas said.

Savannah laughed. "Well, if the *mayor* thinks so . . . " It was dark, but she was still embarrassed to feel her cheeks get hot. She was blushing, and about sixty seconds away from full scale flirting. She had to get away. Glancing at the house, she saw that Mrs. Fuller's window was still lit. She was still awake. Savannah had to get away. She had to talk with someone.

Turning back to Pastor Thomas, she spoke as graciously as she knew how, which was very. "Thank you for walking me home. I do appreciate the kindness. And I hope you will pardon my various missteps. I sometimes speak too . . . freely."

Thomas started to protest, but she held up her hand. "Please," she said. "I really am too free sometimes. I will look forward to Friday," she said. *With great dread*, she added to herself.

Pastor Thomas tipped his hat, and bowed slightly. He disappeared back toward the parsonage, into the dark. Savannah noticed the shape of his shoulders while he was walking away and wondered why she did.

After a few moments staring after him, Savannah walked slowly up to the boardinghouse. She closed the front door behind her quietly and turned sharply to the right in order to cross the hall that led to Mrs. Fuller's room. She could still see the light under the door. She tapped lightly on the door with her knuckles. She and Mrs. Fuller had had many late-night conversations here.

Mrs. Fuller was sitting up in bed, reading, nightcap on, and Savannah took her accustomed place on the settee. "Good evening," she said.

"Good evening," Mrs. Fuller replied. "Something is on your heart, dearie. You can tell me all about it."

"Well, no, I can't," Savannah said. "At least not yet. But I *can* tell you part of it, the part that troubles me so much. And I really need to tell somebody."

Mrs. Fuller put her book on the nightstand.

"What is your trouble, dearie?" Mrs. Fuller called her *dearie* every chance she got.

"There are two parts to this. First, and I don't believe I am imagining anything, all the signs are that Pastor Thomas is . . . after me."

"Well, he would be a fool if he weren't, honey. And he is no fool. How could he not be after you? I thought we put a mirror in your room. Did you break it?"

Savannah hesitated. "Well . . . when you first teased me about him, I said it was impossible. I wasn't being bashful or coy, or anything like that. My problem is that it really is impossible. In ordinary circumstances, I wouldn't mind at all being courted by a man like . . . like him."

"So *he* is not the problem, you are saying."

"Yes, that is right," Savannah replied. "I am the problem."

Mrs. Fuller just waited.

"Apart from his possible interest in me, you would agree that Pastor Thomas is a fine pastor?"

"Yes. He is going to go very far. I wouldn't be surprised if he winds up being king of the Presbyterians some day. Or whatever we call it."

Savannah laughed, in spite of herself. "And because he is a fine pastor, and a fine man, I could not possibly marry him."

Mrs. Fuller nodded. "So I have gathered, dearie. What I have *not* gathered is why you couldn't ever marry him."

Savannah breathed deeply. "I wish I didn't have to tell you this. But I need your help in staving off his . . . *attentions*. If I don't tell you the reason I can't, I know that you would be doing whatever you could to encourage him."

Mrs. Fuller nodded again. "That's right. Quite correct. I would consider it my duty as a mother in Israel."

"Before I moved here—and it was before I became a Christian, too—on my way moving west, I . . . I got involved in a morally compromised situation. I don't want to tell you the details, because it would humiliate me into the ground. But if Pastor Thomas presses his suit past a certain point, I would have to tell him about it. I couldn't withhold it from him then. And no minister with *any* instinct for self-preservation in the ministry would continue to pursue me after I told him what I would have to tell him. And I couldn't bear that." Savannah stopped.

After a moment, she added. "And that is why he needs to be headed off. Or at the very least not encouraged."

Mrs. Fuller sat quietly for a moment, thinking. "I know that nobody talks about this much, honey, but lots of nice girls have been in your position. I don't say it is a trifle, but neither do I say it is an obstacle that can't be got over."

Savannah shook her head, a little impatiently. "Yes, yes, I know that part. I have been out in the world for a few years. I do know that. Lots of men marry women with less than perfect pasts, which is very *nice* of them, since many of them helped to create some of those imperfect pasts."

"But if you know all this, then what is the problem?"

"It is not exactly the fact that he is a minister, although that is part of it. It is more the *kind* of minister he is. If Thomas were doing something else as a vocation, I think I would feel the same way. It is the *kind* of man he is, whatever his vocation."

"Explain yourself, dearie."

"Mrs. Fuller." Savannah stopped and collected her thoughts. "Here is the problem. I know that I could find a man who would marry me. I know that I could find a man that I could tell my past to, and he would accept it, and me along with it. But . . . I think I am going to be a handful."

Mrs. Fuller laughed out loud. "I am glad to see this level of self-awareness in one so young . . ."

"And because I am a handful, I think that only a certain kind of man could marry me and not make me utterly miserable afterward. The kind of man who could marry me and not make me miserable is the kind of man, I think, who could easily be troubled by my past. And I am not saying this to blame him. I think he would have every right to be troubled by it." Toward the end, the words began to gush out.

"I understand." Mrs. Fuller nodded.

"Do you see my dilemma? I don't want a man to be gracious to me because he has low standards. I need one who has high standards, with forgiveness of course being one of them. But forgiveness is one thing and consequences are another. And freedom from the consequences, in the nature of the case, is not something a woman in my position can demand or expect. So the wrong kind of man would make me miserable, but wouldn't find me unmarriageable. The right kind of man could lead me, and protect me . . . and do all the things a husband should do. And he wouldn't make me miserable. He would, however, be likely to take into account the consequences of what I have done. And I think that Pastor Thomas is that kind of man. That second kind of man."

Mrs. Fuller's eyes opened wider than they had been a moment before. "You're in love with him!"

Savannah covered her face with her hands, and said miserably, "I'm a goner."

Mrs. Fuller got out of bed and came to where Savannah was sitting and sat down beside her. She took her hands in hers, and just sat there without saying anything.

After a few moments, Savannah sat up in exasperation. "This is such a small town," she said. "And he is the pastor of my church. There is absolutely nowhere to run, or hide, or anything." Mrs. Fuller patted the back of her hand again. Savannah then added that the mayor had invited Pastor Thomas on his Spokane trip that weekend. "I am going to be in the same *car* with him. For an hour and a half. Each way. Just sitting there, trying to talk across an unbridgeable chasm."

"When did you find out about that?"

"Just now. Pastor Thomas walked me home from Sally's. He told me the mayor had invited him."

"Wait. He just walked you home?"

"Yes. He was very nice . . ."

Mr. Fuller snorted. "I dare say he was very nice. But I am curious. You say *yes* when he asks to walk you home—he did ask, didn't he?—and you say *yes*, delighted, and then after you get home you come in here to ask me to stop trying to get you together? I am going to need at least some help from you, dearie."

NIGHT AT THE DAVENPORT

Much more rational, my dear Caroline, I dare say,
but it would not be near so much like a ball.
JANE AUSTEN, *PRIDE AND PREJUDICE*

Mrs. Fuller came into the boardinghouse loudly, letting the brown and very worn screen door slam. She went into the kitchen to set down her parcel, and then came back out to where Savannah was. It was late afternoon, some time after Savannah was home from school, which is why Savannah was finished grading her papers and sitting by herself in the common living area. "Oh, oh," Mrs. Fuller said. She sat down next to Savannah, flustered and out of breath. "I am all of a doodah," she said.

Savannah had been reading a magazine, which she put down immediately. "Dear, what is it?"

"I did not mean to eavesdrop . . . bless my soul . . . there was nothing I could do about it . . . this just happened to me," she said.

"What are you talking about?" Savannah asked.

"I had left a plate at the picnic by accident, and Hannah—you know Hannah with the freckles?—had told me that it was in the kitchen at the church. So I went there to get it and as I was on my way out—you know that hall by the side door?—I almost walked straight into a conversation between Pastor Thomas and Mr. Lambeth. They were just around the corner. I stopped just in time, but after a moment I realized that the conversation was not for my ears. I didn't know what to do—but they weren't trying to be quiet either, neither of them. I still don't know what to do."

Savannah was immediately more interested than she knew she ought to be, in spite of herself.

"What were they talking about?"

Mrs. Fuller recovered some of her composure, and cocked an eyebrow at Savannah. And it must be said that Mrs. Fuller knew how to cock an eyebrow. "You, dearie."

Savannah tried to act shocked. "Me?"

"Well, it would have been astonishing for them to be talking about anyone or anything else, it seems to me. I have never seen a bowl of potato salad thrown by anyone in finer fettle. Or with better aim."

Savannah laughed out loud. "What were they saying?"

Mrs. Fuller cleared her throat. "Mr. Lambeth had come to demand that Pastor Thomas do something about you. He said that it was unbecoming, to a monstrous degree . . . I don't know why he talks like that . . . to allow a parishioner to be treated as he was treated. In a church with decent standards, as though he knew anything about *those*, he said there would be some form of admonition, some kind of discipline. And Mr. Lambeth had waited patiently for a few weeks to see if something, anything, was going to happen. When it became apparent that Pastor Thomas was neglecting his duties in the most egregious and flagrant way possible, Mr. Lambeth had finally determined to come and confront him about it. 'So what about it?' he said."

"Then Pastor Thomas said, bless him, that under ordinary circumstances he most certainly would have dealt with any member of the church who had thrown a hard object at another member's head—thus far, he and Mr. Lambeth were in agreement—but then he told him that what he had whispered to you had been overheard by others, and he asked Mr. Lambeth if he'd like him to repeat it back to him."

Mrs. Fuller continued, "Well, Mr. Lambeth muttered something that I didn't catch, but I think a *no* was in there somewhere.

"A few seconds passed and then it was Pastor Thomas again. 'In short, Mr. Lambeth, I would be severely disappointed in any female parishioner of mine who didn't throw something at a man who spoke to her like that.'

"Mr. Lambeth muttered some more, and Pastor Thomas said, 'There will be no apology coming to you from Miss Westmoreland. And yes, she knows this. I have spoken with her about the incident. I do not have high hopes, given the manner in which you have come to me today, but there is an apology owed, and so I am now asking on her behalf for an apology to her from you.'

"Then it got silent, and then I heard him threatening Pastor Thomas—said he'd be sorry, that kind of thing. When he was done, Pastor Thomas said, 'Good day, Mr. Lambeth.' I just had time to step through the side door into the Sunday School room there. When Lambeth got to the door of the church, he turned around for what I suppose he thought would be a most severe retort. He said something like, 'It is apparently too much to expect a bachelor pastor to deal appropriately with a beautiful parishioner that he is sweet on. Everybody sees that, you know.'"

"Then Pastor Thomas said, 'Everybody sees that she is beautiful. I think even *you* probably see that. As for being sweet on her, I am not in the habit of confiding anything to men like yourself.'"

He didn't deny anything, Savannah thought. But that doesn't matter, she added to herself. Nothing matters. Don't let it start mattering. But it already matters.

Savannah realized with a start a few moments later that Mrs. Fuller was looking at her, waiting. "So what shall I do?" she said.

"Well, I do think you should tell Pastor Thomas that you overheard them. He will understand. You weren't trying to eavesdrop."

"No, certainly not." Mrs. Fuller looked suitably shocked. "When do you think I should tell him?"

"You aren't planning on telling anyone else about it, are you?"

"No, no." Mrs. Fuller shook her head.

"Then I think it'll wait until Sunday. No sense making a special trip up to the church. That would just make it seem a much bigger issue than it is."

Mrs. Fuller relaxed. "Pastor Thomas didn't deny anything when Lambeth said he was sweet on you."

"Shush," Savannah said. "Out of the question. Just impossible." Savannah was starting to get concerned. She knew Mrs. Fuller well enough to know that the preliminary teasing was just that, preliminary to some more serious conversations. And she did not know what she could say when that happened. She had already spent several sleepless nights going over what she could possibly say. The nights had been sleepless because, beyond what she had already told her, there was nothing she could say.

Friday eventually came. By turns, Savannah felt that the day was rushing toward her and then that it was crawling toward her. Sometimes she thought it was receding. Some moments it would never come, and other times it was almost upon her. So when the mayor's large automobile pulled up at her door around four that afternoon, Savannah had been staring

expectantly out the window and down the street. She
could see that Pastor Thomas was already in the car,
and that he was in the back seat. She waited a few
moments so that it wouldn't seem like she had been
staring out of the window. A moment later she closed
the front door quietly behind her and walked briskly down the front walk, trying to take deep breaths.
There would be no oxygen when she got to the car.

To her great relief, Mr. Martin, who had been in
the front seat with the mayor, hopped out and held
the door for her. She would not be in the back seat
with Pastor Thomas, she thought, with great relief and
greater disappointment. It has to be one or the other,
she said to herself severely. And it *can't* be one of them.

If anyone were to try to guess at her internal commotion from her conversation, that person would have
gone far astray. Savannah felt ludicrous, and as though
she were carrying the load of the entire conversation—
which was not exactly accurate—but from the outside,
she simply appeared vivacious. Mr. Martin was completely bowled over, and quietly extended his full ap-
proval to the mayor's use of this beauty to advertise
the admirable qualities of Paradise. So because it was
the mayor's idea, and because Thomas already ap-
proved, things went very smoothly. Savannah didn't
know that she had such an appreciative audience, but
she had one.

Neither did she know the nature of the appreciation. The mayor was a born booster, and he simply wanted everyone in Spokane to think that all the

schoolteachers in Paradise Valley were as beautiful as Savannah. Everything about Paradise was lovely, and Savannah was a walking metaphor for the mayor's entire project.

Pastor Thomas was an honest Christian, one who had admitted to himself the day before that he was inextricably in love with her. He couldn't close his eyes without seeing her draw herself up to her full height to wind up with the potato salad. He was a naturally confident man, and so there were times when that confidence ruled. He knew they would be together. He just had to pursue her thoughtfully. He could see she was skittish, but he didn't think he was the cause of it. But there *was* a cause of it, and this was what lay behind his alternating bouts of despair. He had an educated guess at the trouble, but he wasn't sure. He had talked with Mr. Felton about it several times, once when he was up and once when he was down. In the meantime he determined that he was just going to enjoy the car ride.

Mr. Martin was fairly new to Paradise. He had been there longer than Pastor Thomas, but not by much, by a year or so. The mayor had almost not invited him, because Martin had become friends with Lambeth already, which the mayor didn't like, but he still thought that Martin was gregarious and outgoing, and that he didn't seem to share in Lambeth's general demeanor of sullenness. His first instinct would have been better.

Martin sat on the driver's side in the back seat, enjoying Savannah's profile every time she turned to say something. He was happy to take life's little gifts as they came, but one time Savannah turned to reply to something Pastor Thomas said, and Todd Martin sat up a little straighter in his seat. Milwaukee. Why was he thinking of Milwaukee? Todd Martin had seen Savannah before.

He was almost sure of it. Or, to be more precise, he alternated between feeling sure of it and being more or less sure of it. But the most he could come up with was an identification with Milwaukee somehow, and he could not figure out why. And that had come to him unbidden when he wasn't trying to figure it out. Now that he was actively trying to remember details, every detail fled from him.

Martin was a salesman, and he traveled a great deal. When he did, he often frequented places a respectable man ought not to frequent, and he had seen things he shouldn't really have seen. In one of his first conversations with Lambeth he had identified himself as a "man of the world," and he was happy to consider himself as such. That was not his full persona in Paradise, of course, but when he was out by himself, traveling from city to city, there was no God within his mouth.

But he was still a good salesman, which meant that he was attentive. He noticed details, and he now noticed that he had seen Savannah somewhere before. He couldn't quite place it, but the first thing that had floated into his mind was Milwaukee—and that city was on his route. He had been there often. Many times, in fact.

That is what made it so difficult. What *hadn't* he seen in Milwaukee?

Pastor Thomas brought something up—something about the look of a barn they had just passed—which took his mind off it for the time being. But he knew that he would return later to puzzle on it.

The mayor then interrupted their general wandering conversation to bring them back to the serious business of boosting. "Now you all are my guests on this trek," he began, "and so you can rest assured that I am not expecting you to say or do anything. Liberty hall. Just enjoy yourselves. But I will say that, if the chance arises, and you have the chance to say that the university has grown in quite a remarkable way since last year, I can tell you that I, for one, would not take it amiss."

The trip flew by, and, contrary to her expectation, Savannah enjoyed herself quite thoroughly. She could interact with Pastor Thomas, but not directly, and she felt safe and comfortable both. She didn't like the way she noticed Mr. Martin glancing at her a few times, but she wasn't entirely sure about what he was doing. But she just had a sense, the way she often did, that a particular man was not the kind of man she wanted to get to know better. He was gregarious enough, and smart enough, and smiled quickly, but the edges of his soul were a little threadbare. Something was not quite together in Mr. Martin.

They pulled into the Davenport about twenty minutes early, and a valet took their car promptly. After it had disappeared around the corner, the mayor presented his arm to Savannah so that she would not have to enter without an escort. Pastor Thomas and Todd Martin walked behind them, chatting easily. Thomas had noticed that something was off with Martin, in a way similar to what Savannah had, but because he was in a different position than she was, his thoughts had turned naturally to evangelism.

As they walked through the doors and came into the lobby, Thomas was taken aback in spite of himself. He had not seen anything this ornate for several years, and certainly not west of the Mississippi. Money in the form of silver had poured out of the mountains to the east, back over in Idaho, and much of it had settled here in this lobby. The ceiling was richly and intricately carved. The hall was huge, and crowded with dazzling people. Off to the left Savannah could see a thick line of people wending their way to what she assumed was the ballroom. The fact there was a ball was almost an afterthought, giving people an excuse to dress up in their finery in order to display it all in the Marie Antoinette room. That was the ostensible occasion, but the main lobby was crowded with politicians and businessmen and ladies, and women who three hundred years before would have been ladies-in-waiting, and numerous waiters with trays full of drinks working their way through the crowd. When the mayor saw them all visiting below, and heard the music from the ballroom, he beamed and breathed in deeply, as much as to tell the others, "This is why I was born."

They all made their way down into the crowd. When they were on the edge of that crowd, Todd Martin immediately disappeared, like a hare into tall grass. A moment later the mayor, having seen some important personages across the room, politely excused himself. This left Savannah with Thomas, as though they were a couple.

Savannah then turned to Pastor Thomas and very politely said, "Your company has been most engaging and delightful, but please don't feel any obligation to serve as an escort for me." She then added, "I have been to such events before." She didn't say "and can take care of myself, thank you" but she might as well have. That fact became apparent to her as soon as she spoke, and so she did say, "That sounded rude, which I did not intend. I simply meant that I did not wish to lay any claim to your company, for I have no claim on it."

Pastor Thomas smiled. "Perhaps I can propose a solution to our dilemma?"

Savannah smiled back in spite of herself. "You may."

"I hear from the music that the dancing has started. Why don't I ask you to come dance with me now? That way I can discharge what you are assuming must be an irksome burden for me, and after that we go our separate ways down into that crowd, where you can fend for yourself. That way you don't feel you have imposed unduly on my time, and I don't feel like I have neglected my responsibility for your well-being."

Savannah laughed. "I accept your solution, very handsomely offered." She was now flirting, and she knew it. But so was he, and it was all still quite impossible, and she was furiously unhappy with her very happy self. He offered his arm, and she took it. The line winding into the ballroom had thinned out, so they had no trouble making their way in. The ballroom was enormous, and there was more than enough room for all the couples who wanted to dance. The room was full but not crowded. The orchestra was at the far end and was playing a stately waltz.

Pastor Thomas turned and bowed to her, and assumed the correct position for the dance. He noted her look of surprise, and laughed. "I'm a Presbyterian," he said. "Not a Primitive Baptist."

"Well, that works out," she said. "I'm a Presbyterian too."

"I know," he said. "I've seen you at church."

They stopped speaking as they moved into the dance, and she noted—not that she was surprised at anything anymore—that he was a very smooth dancer. She danced well, too, but had to pay close attention. He moved confidently, leading her easily. She could feel his muscled shoulder through his jacket. I am in very bad trouble, she thought.

The dance was over far more quickly than she wanted, and she found herself curtsying to his bow, both of them feeling very old-fashioned, and taking his arm again to be led out to the lobby where she was to be jettisoned, abandoned, forsaken. He knows what he is doing to me, he *must*. When they got to the floor, he turned and bent his head slightly and said, "I will see you soon," and disappeared. She stared after him for a moment, very much in turmoil, and then turned around with a sigh.

When she did so she almost ran into Mr. Brent Watkins from Pullman. He was part owner of the grain silos there, and he lived close enough to Paradise for him to be something of an affliction to Savannah. He beamed at her. "Well, well," he said. "I was wondering if you would be here, and when I saw you across the way, I came straight over. We are small town pals, right? We have to stick together at these big city events."

Savannah smiled, despaired a little inside, tried to be brave, and said that yes, she supposed so. Mr. Watkins was a cheerful, flirtatious, oblivious soul, immune to any kind of brush off that was not entirely rude. He had been working up his courage to ask Savannah out on a date for over a year, but until his shipment of courage arrived, he had contented himself with cornering her at public events in order to be old friends with her. Savannah was standing where she could see the ornate clock on the balcony, and she despaired a little more. Mr. Watkins was nothing if not garrulous. He sought to cover up his nervousness with a slather of words, and because of his acute awareness of her beauty, he was very nervous.

She was a kind woman, and he was the kind of insecure and outgoing fellow that she could not figure out how to dismiss without crushing. The only thing to do, as she had discovered on previous occasions, was to give him a respectable amount of time before beginning her efforts at disentanglement. She very carefully allowed her gaze to slide over the clock on the balcony again, and was dismayed to see that it seemed to be running backward, like Hezekiah's sun dial. Her choice was stark—this tedious interval at the party or unkindness to this poor man. She resigned herself to her usual pattern. Only one thing could make this circumstance more awkward for her, she thought . . .

The voice of Pastor Thomas broke in suddenly, gloriously, irritatingly. "Good evening, Mr. Watkins," he said cheerfully, shaking his hand. "Good to see you. I am very sorry, but I am afraid I have to whisk Miss Westmoreland off. Can you ever forgive me?"

Mr. Watkins smiled. "Certainly," he said. He was about to ask why she had to be whisked off, but decided against it. Long experience had taught him that that kind of question was a risky one.

Pastor Thomas presented his arm to Savannah confidently, just as he had done before. Feeling as though she had lost another round, Savannah took his arm with seething gratitude. She had been losing in the Mr. Watkins situation also, but the only thing at stake there was twenty minutes or so. She was by this time very aware of the fact that Thomas was staking far more than that, and that she couldn't respond to him and that she very much wanted to.

As soon as they were some distance away, Savannah said, "So why did I need to be whisked away?"

"So that you might be rescued," Thomas said. "By me."

"Rescued from poor Mr. Watkins? I didn't need your help for that. But thank you for your thoughtfulness." Savannah tried, unsuccessfully, to keep the indignation out of her voice.

Thomas nodded. "Well, I know that I could be wrong about it, but it certainly seemed that way to me. Whenever I see you talking to an unmarried man, I simply assume that you need to be rescued promptly."

Savannah colored, and looked the other way

"I had only your best interests in mind," he said, with apparent meekness. It was only apparent. He was acting.

Her indignation came up into her throat. "Well, Pastor Thomas, whatever your motives, I think it was highly presumptuous . . . "

He broke in, solicitously. "I am more than willing to make full restitution. All we need do is cross the hall, speak for a few moments, and then I will escort you back to Mr. Watkins again."

"No, no . . ." she said, without thinking. Not back to Mr. Watkins. And so then her will collapsed completely and she meekly submitted. "Thank you for rescuing me."

"You are most welcome."

"But I will remember this." She had meekly submitted a moment ago, but it had just been for the moment. Her words fell to the floor like leaden bluster.

The rest of the event remained as much an event as it had been when they arrived, but because of the long drive back to Paradise, they decided to leave before any of the Spokane people were ready to leave. The crowd was still a crowd, and was surging cheerfully back and forth like a large lake on a choppy day. The four of them made their way up the stairs, up the bank of the lake, and then back out to their waiting car, with Mr. Martin acting like he was a little bit worse for wear. When they got to the car, he stopped them all with his right hand in the air and he said, quite apologetically, and with a little bit of a slur, that he was very sorry to inconvenience anybody, but could he please have the front seat on the way back? He was feeling a trifle woozy, and that road had some hellacious curves in it, he said, and he sometimes didn't do too well with that kind of thing when he had been enjoying himself.

Pastor Thomas acceded gladly, and Savannah did so somewhat grimly. She felt like she should have been able to handle Pastor Thomas, but that larger forces were conspiring against her. But the first half hour of the drive was peaceful, and the conversation matched it. There was only an occasional comment, and things were not nearly as animated as they had been on the drive up. The hum of the tires was very soothing, and the snatches of murmured conversation here and there seemed to fit somehow, and so Savannah made her peace with being where she was, and settled comfortably in her seat. The car was warm and she leaned her head back against the seat.

A jolt startled her awake. That jolt was the car coming to a stop, and she sat up slowly. She recognized her house. They were home. That was fast. And then she realized with horror that she had been fast asleep on Pastor Thomas' shoulder. "Oh, oh," she said. "I am so sorry. You should have said something."

"I didn't want to," he said.

MILWAUKEE

He that covereth a transgression seeketh love;
But he that repeateth a matter separateth very friends.

PROVERBS 17:9

Todd Martin had made fast friends with Alan Lambeth, or at least that's the way he initially thought of it. Alan Lambeth knew that Martin felt like he was hitting it off with him, and so he allowed him to think that. He was accustomed to the pattern, and could be very charming in his way. Many men had been put off their guard by it, and Todd Martin had just recently joined them.

Martin was in Lambeth's office now, leaning back in the wooden bank chair, one leg resting on the other.

He had sandy hair, brushed straight back, and a pair of spectacles that he wore like he didn't need them. He was a salesman, and he looked like a salesman. He had an affable face, one that didn't mind spending time with you, and didn't mind a couple of shades of dishonesty. Nothing black though. Gray tints were acceptable.

He was chattering aimlessly, as he sometimes did, and mentioned that he thought he had seen that Miss Westmoreland somewhere before, and was pretty sure it was Milwaukee. And he was starting to say that he thought it was in a pretty seedy place, not at all like her respectable position now, when he caught a glimpse of a sudden hard gaze from Lambeth. It frightened him somehow, and it did so in a way he didn't under-stand at all. Martin was a scamp, and something of a scoundrel, but he wasn't rotten clean through the way Lambeth was. He had some boundaries, or at least he thought he did. He had done some bad things in his time, but was not yet a thoroughly bad man. On a fran-tic impulse, he suddenly decided to play dumb, but he wasn't exactly sure why.

"What do you mean?" Lambeth wanted to know.

"Oh, it's all vague," Martin said. "I am pretty sure I have seen her before . . . that part's not vague. In sales you have to have a good eye for faces, and her face is a good one to have a good eye for." He laughed un-certainly, trying to get the conversation back to where it was before. "As for the seedy part, well, that's just the kind of places I go to—especially in Milwaukee. I know I didn't see her in church."

"Because I don't go to church," he added, a moment later.

Lambeth just stared at him for a moment, and then sat back in his chair, apparently relaxing. The conversation was back where Martin thought he wanted it to be. But Lambeth had seen immediately that Martin had been spooked by something somehow, and that trying to get anything more from him right now would be vain, or even counterproductive. Maybe he could get more later. Maybe he could just use what information had come out. Milwaukee had a promising feel.

Martin really had been spooked. *Badly.* He tried to sort it out later in his mind. Lambeth's eyes were dark to begin with, but in *that* moment there had seemed to be layers of black malice going all the way down. Martin was not big into unspoken meanings, but there had been plenty of unspoken meaning in that stare. Martin hadn't thought of God for years, but now, for some reason, that was exactly what his mind started doing.

He decided later on that he had realized in that moment, somehow, that if you looked into eyes like that long enough, a time would come when you would be looking out of eyes like that. He had started to grasp the kind of things that Lambeth would be willing to do, and he saw instantly, and was not quite sure how, that if he didn't break with Lambeth, he would be doing those same sorts of things too. And he knew that he had absolutely no desire to be like that. He refused to be someone like that. He certainly didn't feel like he had decided anything. He felt decided upon. It was more like some kind of strange revolt had overtaken him from behind.

Their conversation recovered somewhat. Martin took—and Lambeth let him take—their conversation back to the business that had brought Martin in to see Lambeth in the first place. Martin lived east of town on a forty-acre piece, and they were planning an easement that would prove itself to be an unpleasant surprise to one of Martin's neighbors. But Lambeth had friends in city government, in particular a gent named Jensen, and the thing was going to happen, surprise or no surprise, pleasant or unpleasant. Martin slid back into ordinary dishonesty, and it felt like coming home. It felt like virtue.

When Martin left half an hour later, his mind kept returning to that stare, that moment. He thought of God again, and swore at himself. What good does that do? But two minutes later, he was doing the same thing, and he swore again. Nothing like a glimpse of the devil to make a man religious, he thought.

Three days later, Savannah was looking out the window of the schoolhouse, preparing her bundle of paper and books to carry home. She was startled to see Alan Lambeth walking up the front walk to the school. By this time—it was late afternoon—no one else was around, and in a few moments she heard his boots clacking down the hallway toward her classroom. She had no idea why he was there, and was glad she had seen him coming. She was braced and composed for whatever he might be there for, and after she had prayed a very quick prayer, she felt herself completely at peace. She did not know why she was at peace. That didn't make much sense at all, but she was glad for it.

He stepped into her classroom quietly, and shut the door behind him. "Good afternoon," he said.

She nodded, not quite prepared to say anything yet. She was looking at him intently, trying to read him. She wasn't sure, but thought he was smirking.

"I suppose you don't know why I have come here today," he finally said.

"I can't imagine," she replied. "Unless it is to apologize for what you called me at the picnic. But if that were the case, I doubt if you would have begun by making me guess."

Lambeth laughed, coldly. "No, you are right," he said. "I didn't come to do that."

Savannah stood quietly. The peace was settling in around her. She didn't know why it was there, but she certainly welcomed it gladly. She knew something bad was coming, and was grateful that her nerves were not reacting as though something bad were coming.

"I came," Lambeth said, "to tell you that I know all about Milwaukee." He was watching her intently as he said this, and was immediately disappointed. He couldn't see any reaction in her. She didn't flush, or turn white, or gasp. She just stood there.

"I have certainly been there," she said. "But since you appear to believe that it is highly significant, suppose you tell me what you know about Milwaukee. Why should that be significant to me?"

Lambeth knew that Martin's memory for faces was reliable, and believed that Martin knew something definite that he had decided at the last minute not to say. Lambeth had decided to try to bluff the information out of Savannah because it had seemed like a reasonable bet to him at the time. He had not reckoned with the peace of God, which passeth all understanding, the peace that guardeth hearts and minds.

He had nothing more to say, and he knew it. And now she knew that he was bluffing, and knew that his knowledge of her past was somehow limited to the word *Milwaukee*. But how had he come by that word?

"No need to tell you," he said. "I just wanted to see if you would acknowledge it."

"I freely acknowledge having been there, and can see no reason for denying that. I acknowledge also taking the train from there to Spokane when I first moved out here. But beyond that, I don't believe I need to acknowledge anything in pursuit of what you might mean by your cryptic guesses. And I don't believe you know anything besides that one word."

No sense pretending. She was certainly sharp. So he grinned at her, with a malevolent leer. "But I will."

And with that he was gone, out the door and down the hall. The peace of God that had enveloped her during their entire conversation seemed to have gone down the hall with him. Savannah sat down at her desk, badly rattled. Someone must have said something to him. But who could possibly . . .?

Martin. He was a traveling salesman. And he had just been with them on the trip up to the Davenport. Had she said anything at all about Milwaukee? Lambeth had to have gotten hold of the word Milwaukee just recently. If he had known anything more than just the name of the city, it would have been the perfect thing to whisper at the picnic. But he hadn't done that, which means he hadn't known it then. It had to be Martin. He was charming, and sleazy, and low rent, and also charming. She began cudgeling her mind, trying to think if she had ever seen Martin before. But he was a nondescript salesman, and she was a strikingly beautiful woman. When it came to remembering faces, he had a distinct advantage over her, although that part of the challenge did not occur to Savannah.

Savannah just sat at her desk, staring at the back wall of her classroom. She had instantly seen that there was no need to try to figure out what to do from the very straightforward fact that there was nothing to do. All she could do was pray. Had it come to that? Just pray, just pray. Why had Lambeth been allowed to take her peace away with him? She was grateful that she had had that peace as long as it had lasted—she had not reacted to him at all. *That* had to have been a little unsettling to him. She knew that she hadn't reacted because all the reactions had happened to her after he had left the room. He must think her a cool customer, at any rate.

Walking back to the bank, Lambeth found himself in the grip of a furious energy that was not going to be denied. He had to find out what Martin was referring to. His words to Savannah—"but I will"—took on a frantic necessity. At the same time, he couldn't *look* frantic. He couldn't look eager. Patience. He breathed deeply. He knew instinctively—suddenly, right then he realized—that it was his sudden cold intensity that had caused Martin to clam up the way he had. He should have just let him chatter on, making small talk.

Lambeth walked back into his office at the bank with a clatter and bustle, and tried to make it seem like it was all business. And in this he succeeded—he was like this a lot, and the tellers and staff out in the front thought it was all business. He slammed a couple of drawers in his desk just to put a finishing touch on it.

He knew that Martin was heading out for another one of his sales tours the day after tomorrow. And he also knew what no one else did, which is that Martin would frequently take a day or two off before he had to leave for a sales trip. He would go out on the mountain, or on the ridge south of town, in order to hunt, or fish. If he had been a spiritual man, he would have prayed, but as it was, Martin never prayed.

After pondering late into the evening, Lambeth saddled his horse early next morning, and rode out to the northeast of town, the route he knew that Martin always took to the mountain. He waited patiently for about forty-five minutes, letting his horse graze quietly by the side of the path. No one ever came out this way, especially in the early morning. Looking up, he saw another horseman coming, and he recognized Martin's hat first.

He got back on his horse, and sat in what he knew to be a cold and threatening posture. It was not as if he looked as though he was going to draw his pistol. But it did look as though he was a bearer of grim tidings, which he was.

Martin rode up. "Alan," he said, nodding.

"Morning," Lambeth replied. "I wanted to catch you before your trip, and I figured you would come out here now the way you usually do."

"Well, all right then," Martin said. "What's it about?" He already knew what it was about. He knew what that look on Lambeth's face had meant when he suddenly, for reasons he did not yet fully understand, decided to shut up about Savannah.

"Well, I happen to know that you know something about our Miss Westmoreland and her time in Milwaukee. And I know that you decided on the spur of the moment to blur it over for me. That much was obvious to me. I don't know why you don't want to tell me the whole thing, but you spontaneously decided you didn't want to do that. Isn't that right? Now there is no explaining this—we have always been open with each other, haven't we? I would say that I am hurt, except I am not. But I am most interested in what you might have to tell me."

Martin just sat on the back of his horse, mulling it over. "Go on," he said after a minute.

"Well, you know my style. What I need to get I need to get, but I am not in a rush. I wanted to give you some time to think it over. This trip of yours tomorrow, what is it? Two weeks? When you get back in town, I want to have a little conversation with you, and at the end of that conversation I want to know a lot more about Milwaukee than I do now. On this trip, I want you to think over all the creative ways I could make you wish you had told me what it was. Think it over slowly, Martin. Think about it carefully. Ponder it when you are drifting off to sleep. Think about me when you walk along the road, when you lie down, and when you rise up."

"I believe I understand you," Martin said. He wanted Lambeth to think he was likely to cooperate. At the same time, he did not know how it came about that he had decided never to cooperate, but that was in fact the case. He had always been an easy, greasy, superficial man, but now . . . now he simply loathed Lambeth, and he was not sure where his sudden resolve had come from. He didn't know where his insight had come from. Before he had seen that look of cold fire when Lambeth interrupted him, he had been more than willing to do shady deals with a successful businessman who was what Martin liked to call "realistic." But there was now something else involved, or just now visible and apparent, and Martin had decided somewhere, somehow, to get as far away from it as he possibly could. But he said, evenly enough, "I do want to think it over. Just out of principle. But you know I am a reasonable man."

"Well, let us hope so," Lambeth said, and wheeled his horse around.

Martin spent the day mulling over his options, and didn't see how he had very many. He knew that Lambeth was hard and ruthless, and would probably stick at nothing. He could just get on the train, and never come back, and that seemed at various times to be the best option. But he did not want to crawl, and he liked living in Paradise. He was on the dishonest side of the honesty/dishonesty line, but he had never gotten too far over that line. He had never gone in for genuine mayhem, of the kind that could land him in prison, and that is what it seemed to him that Lambeth was going to be up to.

Moreover, he liked Savannah. He had only met her that one trip up to Spokane, the trip when he had remembered her from Milwaukee. He was vaguely glad that she had made something out of her life, and wasn't stuck back there. If she could get out, why couldn't he get out? She went to church too, he knew that. God again.

Another option was to warn Savannah. If he did that, and then refused Lambeth when he got back, someone else would then know if something happened to him. But what could she do about it? Nothing really. But still he liked the idea of warning her, even if it only gave him an opportunity to talk to her, while seeming somewhat brave and courageous, which might leave a better impression than the last time she saw him, when he was slightly drunk and in danger of being sick.

A third option was to tell Lambeth what he knew. After the first rush of courage had seeped out of his boots—that happened on the ride back to town—he found himself returning to that option more often than he would have liked. But he had no appetite for doing serious harm to anyone, and he could only guess what Lambeth would do with the kind of information he had. Martin hadn't been at the picnic, but he had heard about the potato salad incident, some of it from Lambeth himself, and so he knew that the response from Lambeth, when it happened, would not be proportional at all. Lambeth was the kind of man who lost his temper down deep inside. When Lambeth lost his temper, nobody knew where it had gotten to.

He couldn't do something like that to Savannah, and so he tried to feel noble about it—but just wound up laughing at himself. He would tell her, and then figure out how to deal with Lambeth. He would leave Paradise if he had to. He was catching his train first thing in the morning. He thought he could figure out a way to talk to her at her home on his way to the train station. Nobody could see him because it would be early enough that nobody was likely to. A large lilac hedge separated the boardinghouse from the neighbors on the side of the house where Savannah slept. He was pretty sure where her room was from a comment someone had made when he'd been invited to dinner at the boardinghouse a few months before. He could just toss a couple of pebbles against her window. If she didn't answer, he had tried, and if she did, he could tell her and be away.

And so that is exactly what he did. The next morning, the street was quiet, entirely quiet, when Martin walked quietly up to the house. He still had plenty of time for the train, and in fact had even come a little earlier than he'd needed to in order to ensure that the street would be really quiet. It was going to be a warm day, but it was early enough in the morning that Martin could feel the first bite of fall. He stooped and picked up a few pebbles from the street, and then walked across the dew-covered lawn. Other than disturbing a robin hunting for worms, all was quiet. He tossed one of the pebbles at what he was pretty sure was Savannah's window.

He waited for a moment, and then tossed another pebble. A second after the fourth pebble, he saw the curtain moving slightly, and he stopped. An eye peered out from between the curtains, blinked, and disappeared. A minute went by, and then the curtains were pulled back and Savannah appeared in the window with a robe on. She then pulled the window up, gently, and stooped down. "Mr. Martin!" she said.

"May I come closer?" he said. "I don't want to speak loudly."

"Certainly," she said. "Although I admit myself a bit surprised."

"I will just be a moment . . . I have to catch a train."

So he told her. He tried not to be melodramatic, and was mostly successful in that. He told her that he had recognized her from Milwaukee, and that he had let that slip in a conversation with Lambeth, and that

Lambeth had frightened him by how he had jumped on it. "Like a duck on a June bug," Martin said. He told her that Lambeth had given him to the end of this next sales trip to tell him everything he knew. He had acted like he was going to, but—he wanted Savannah to know—he wasn't ever going to. He said that Lambeth may have already tried to bully her with it—"He did," Savannah said—and she should know that all Lambeth knows is the word Milwaukee, and that is all he is ever going to know.

"I haven't decided yet whether I am coming back from my little trip. If I do, it will be because I think I have figured out what I can try to do with Lambeth. If I don't figure it out, then maybe I got homesick for Vermont. Whatever the case, I wanted you to know there was nothing to worry about."

Savannah was strangely serene about Mr. Martin knowing about her past secret—there was the peace of God again—and thanked him sincerely. When he left, she closed the window and curtains, and sat on the edge of her bed. So Martin knew. It distressed her, but not as deeply as she might have thought it would.

And Martin would have been quite right about there being nothing to worry about if Lambeth had not gone into work very early that same morning. He was driving down Third toward downtown when, glancing over to the left, he saw Martin stepping into the alley behind the boardinghouse where Savannah lived. That was an unmistakable gait. Martin was looking down and didn't see him.

THE NIGHT
OF THE FIRE

What you lose in the fire, you will find amongst the ashes.

FRENCH PROVERB

Martin went on his sales trip—and it was a remarkably profitable trip, his best ever—and about halfway through it he decided he was going to return to Paradise. But it has to be said that he returned on tenterhooks. His first day back, he went straight to Lambeth's office, sat in the chair across from his desk, and told him flat out that he didn't like the game, and wasn't going to say anything more about it.

Lambeth didn't argue. He just looked down at the papers on his desk that he had been working on when

Martin came in. "Get out," he said, and without a word Martin did so.

He had been puzzling a good deal over the fact that Martin had gone to Savannah. He wasn't expecting that, and didn't know what to make of it. He didn't know what had happened in Milwaukee, and apparently Savannah and Martin both did. Now they *both* knew what Savannah had guessed when he had tried to bluff her, which was that he knew nothing but one word, and that he had gotten that word from Martin. But he did know one thing more than this, and that was that Savannah had some sort of secret that was worth protecting. But Martin had talked to her. Was it to warn her in case something happened to him? Was it to coordinate a response in case he found out? Had they been partners in some kind of criminal enterprise? Lambeth shook his head.

He noticed Martin's cap sitting on the chair next to the one he had just been sitting in. It was a small bowler hat, quite distinctive and old-fashioned. He walked around his desk, picked it up and turned it over in his hands. There, on the hat band inside, was a pronounced scrawl. T.M. That will do nicely, Lambeth thought. Not sure what, but it will do it nicely.

Lambeth went home for dinner that evening still pondering. He needed an event that would put Todd Martin into enough trouble that he would know where it came from, and he needed to have an event—ideally the same event—that would show up Savannah somehow. He fried a steak for himself mechanically and sat alone at his kitchen table chewing that same steak just as mechanically. By the time he was done with the steak, he knew what he was going to do. And as soon as he knew, he knew also that he was going to do it soon. No reason for sitting around.

So late that same night, Lambeth made his way down the alley, carrying a collection of oily rags and a can of pitch that he'd rummaged out of his garage. The moon was riding high, although all that appeared to the eye was a slender crescent. It was one in the morning, and the town was entirely quiet and completely still. His plan was a simple one—he was going to set fire to the back of Savannah's boardinghouse, leave Martin's hat there, wait back at the bank for ten minutes or so "working late" as he had been doing just a few moments before. That would not be suspicious because he often worked late like that, and everybody knew it.

He was a very intelligent man, but also a very proud and conceited one. It was not a slight prideful vanity, but a corrosive and acidic pride, the kind that would degrade any intelligence that tried to hold it like a container. The pride had eaten through, and since the day of the picnic the container had started leaking, and Lambeth was now making mistakes.

He had assumed from a stray comment of one of the boarders that he knew where Savannah's room was—on the left side of the house facing the street. He had also seen which side of the house Martin had come from when he entered the alley. He had already checked out where a ladder was stored, across the alley, hanging on the back of a garage, and he was going to prop that against the roof of the porch that ran around the house on three sides. That would be a random dead end for the sheriff to puzzle over.

He would be raising a racket the entire time, and by the time he was at Savannah's window, the rest of the house would be roused, and he would help her to safety. He was not fool enough to believe that this would affect her affections in any way, but at least it would *show* her. He could not win her heart, as he well knew, but he was pretty sure he could have an impact on her heart. What he wanted to do was leave a rude dent in it.

After that episode in the park, he knew he had no chance to win her—he was not trying to win a woman anymore, but was rather trying to win his pride back. He found himself muttering to himself again. The point of this exercise was not to win her, but rather to show her. He would save her life, or at least it would plausibly seem so to other people, and she would be annoyed by it, and that would be a sufficient salve for the blister on his ego. A sufficient salve for the time being.

Lambeth had initially thought of giving this task to Smitty, one of his thugs from the silver mines up north, who was reliable for any kind of dirty work, but pride made him unwilling to let Smitty know that Savannah had gotten under his skin. For she had, in fact, gotten under his skin, and Smitty was the kind of person who would see something like that right away. Smitty was born casting glances sideways.

Finding a few broken pallets across the alley, Lambeth dragged them over and quietly propped them against the back of the house. He looked back and forth, up and down the alley, and then smeared the pitch over the rags and stuffed them down underneath the pallets. He didn't just feel alone; he knew with a dead certainty that he was alone. He placed Martin's hat carefully, made to look as though it had been carelessly set aside for a moment. A few moments later, he struck a match, waited until he was sure it had caught, and then walked across the alley and into a cross alley that would take him a full block away.

Getting to the end of that alley, he turned sharply right and made his way over to the bank where he had kept the light on. That light often burned late, and no one who saw it would think anything of it this time.

Lambeth let himself in the back door of the bank, comfortable in the assurance that the shadows had hidden him well enough. He went to his desk and spent the next ten minutes doodling furiously. When he thought his time there had been well spent, he got up, turned down the light, and exited the front door briskly. He pocketed the keys to the bank, and started to walk decisively down the street to his home, which would take him right past the boardinghouse. When he got to the alley running to the back of the house, he was going to glance down that alley—he had it all planned out—and notice the flickering glow that no doubt would be there by this time.

That was what he was going to do, but what he actually did instead of that was step on a rotten board near the top of the steps that went down to the street level from the bank. The board snapped in two, and Lambeth's leg went straight through. And he then heard a second ominous snap. It was his tibia.

The pain shot up his back and knocked his hat off. Actually it was his fall that did that, but it felt like the pain had done it. Lambeth fell forward, his broken leg trapped by the broken step. He lay still for a moment, collected his breath, and started to move. He almost screamed. He was bound to that place as tightly as if the porch had seized him by both his feet. He couldn't free his good leg without excruciating pain in the bad leg, and the bad leg couldn't go first because that would involve trying to use it. He finally gave up trying, and just lay on the ground, dismally watching the orange glow from the fire he had set. At the end, he didn't know if he'd slept, or had passed out, or some combination of the two.

He was found, hours later, just before dawn, and was taken immediately to Dr. Gritman's house. Some men were returning home after fighting the fire, and they were astonished beyond measure at finding a second emergency on the same night. One of them fetched a stretcher, and the other two lifted Lambeth very gently from his wooden trap, his sidewalk prison. When they got him to the clinic, one of them waited until the doctor arrived, while the others left. Lambeth was shivering under a wool blanket, but managed to ask—despite his chattering teeth—what had happened down the street.

"As I lay there," Lambeth said, "I heard shouting, which was odd for the middle of the night."

"Ah," said the man, whose name was Bill. "Odd it were. The boardinghouse caught fire from the back somewheres. After we got there, we got the fire put out pretty quick. That back porch is going to have to be re-built, and poor old Mrs. Warner, who lived in the back bedroom, was done in by the smoke. But other than that, the house is intact."

Lambeth was crazy with curiosity. The town was deserted, the streets were absolutely silent that time of night. There should have been more than the porch gone. "Who gave out the alarm?" he said. It seemed like a natural question.

"Oh, that was Pastor Thomas," said Bill. "You know, the new Presbyterian one."

Lambeth was just looking at him, eyebrows arched upwards. "What was he doing?"

"He said he was working late on a sermon, and his brain got fuzzled. So he took a walk to clear his head, like. And as he was walking down the street, he saw a glow in the back alley and raised up the hue and cry. Folks were calling him a hero and all, but he said all he did was yell and bang on the front door."

Lambeth hid his exasperation. Martin's hat was still there in the back alley. The sheriff would find it. He would not have the satisfaction of "rescuing" Savannah, to her great distaste and his enjoyment, but the central point of it all was still on course. And Mrs. Warner was dead, which would make it plenty hot for Martin.

The break was a clean one, no complications, and Dr. Gritman had no trouble setting it and applying the cast. "Eight weeks of hobbling for you," the doctor said. "But other than that, it doesn't look to me like you'll have any trouble afterward. So do all your limping now."

Lambeth was back at work a couple days later, and it was a day after that when Sheriff Barnes dropped into the bank. "You have a minute, Lambeth?"

He dropped his papers easily, and said, "Certainly. Could you get the door behind you? Then you can ask anything you want. I am not as agile as I was two weeks ago."

The sheriff didn't like Lambeth that much, but they had a decent working relationship. He sat down comfortably.

"After all the excitement of the other night, it took a while for everything to calm down. But the fire chief tells me the fire at the boardinghouse was most certainly arson, and so I have opened up a case on the unfortunate affair. And because of Mrs. Watson dying, the case is a serious one."

Lambeth nodded at him to go on.

"Now the night of the fire, I understand that you were . . . somewhat incommoded. Would that be a fair way of putting it?"

Lambeth smiled grimly. "I was entirely incommoded."

"When did that happen?"

Lambeth knew when the fire had started, for he had started it, and so was careful to have his leg broken a couple of hours before that. "I usually work late, and that night had quit shortly before midnight. I headed out the way I usually do, and snap, there I was."

"Didn't you yell?"

"I most certainly did. But no one lives close enough apparently. And no one came by. I am sure the doctor told you how they found me. I couldn't crawl or lift myself. And I am sure I passed out a few times, and maybe I even slept a few times. The most miserable night of my life, I can assure you."

Lambeth hesitated. He didn't want to look like he wanted to say anything. He wanted to look like he didn't want to say anything. "I did see something, I think. I thought I saw a man walking down to the boardinghouse, down the alley behind the bank. I remember it because it was the one time I tried to cry out after someone particular. It was dark in the shadows back there, but I thought I recognized Todd Martin."

The sheriff sat a little straighter in his chair. Martin? The hat. "What time was that?" he asked.

"I honestly have no idea. It was before the fire, I know that. But other than that, no idea."

"Martin didn't hear you?"

"Didn't act like it. He just disappeared into the shadows, heading south."

"Why didn't he hear you?"

"I suspect my voice was just croaking by that time. It was hard for me to tell. And I didn't see him until he was a good bit away. But it was Martin all right. That hat of his is hard to mistake. Even if you are seeing things, which I may have been by that point." Lambeth wondered if he was overplaying his hand, but he was in the game all the way by this point.

It seemed to go over well enough. "Right," the sheriff said. "That hat is kind of unmistakable." The sheriff was deep in thought and Lambeth thought it best to leave it there.

When the sheriff showed up to interview Martin, he had Martin's hat in his hand. That fact rattled Martin because it revealed to him how far Lambeth was willing to go in retaliation—trying to frame him on an arson and manslaughter charge. As soon as he had missed his hat, and remembered where it was, he knew that Lambeth would do something bad with it. But *this*?

But in another sense, Martin was not rattled at all, and smiled to himself. Lambeth was not as fully competent as he wanted to appear, and should have done some checking first. Martin had spent the entire night of the fire playing poker with some old friends in Lewiston. His four friends and the barkeep would all be able to vouch for him, having been looking straight at him for that entire night. It was a monthly meeting, and Lambeth should have been a bit more careful. He thought that if Martin was not off on a business trip, he must be "in town," and if in town, then vulnerable.

Martin decided to come back hard. "I don't have any idea how my hat got there. I forgot it in Lambeth's

office a little while ago. But as for it supposedly falling off my head there at the fire, I am afraid I have the
most ironclad alibi you have ever heard of. And that
is unusual because most nights I wouldn't have any
alibi at all. Most nights I am home by myself reading.
But on *that* night I was down in Lewiston all night
playing poker in the presence of scores of people.
And I would guess that a good half of them are even
reliable witnesses."

The sheriff smiled. He knew the saloon. He would
check, but this was interesting. Either Lambeth was
lying, or he had been seeing things, or someone who
looked like Martin was the arsonist and had somehow
come into possession of Martin's hat. And Martin had
brought up leaving his hat in Lambeth's office without
knowing what Lambeth had told him about what he
had seen. The sheriff felt that he was developing a genuine mystery, and he was deeply grateful for it. Most
of what he had to deal with was open and shut, just like
the cell door closing on the drunks he usually housed
overnight. This was a real case. The boys down in Boise couldn't laugh at him for this one. And his family
back East who laughed at him for being sheriff in a
town out west where nothing happened . . . well, now
he could tell them about something that happened. He
would have to wait until it was over, of course.

Martin was sitting calmly in the middle of a cloud
of new purpose. He had been a drifter, a grifter, and
a waster for a number of years. He had been fritter-
ing with his life, and he had always known it on some

level. Now the depth of Lambeth's hostility surprised him, startled him completely, and he found that he was fully awake as a result. It occurred to him that he might die in this part of his story, and he was more than a little interested in the fact that he didn't think he would mind. Far better this than to ramble aimlessly for a few more decades and then shove off in the middle of some card game that he was cheating in.

The most important thing, he thought momentarily, was that if he died, Savannah would have to know somehow that he had not said a word about anything. He would not say a word. Never, not after seeing that look in Lambeth's eyes. He had looked straight down a well of hatred and was astonished with himself how much he had hated it. He would not drink a drop of it. The whole thing felt vaguely religious to him, and he was not sure what to make of that. He wished he could talk to somebody about it, someone like that Pastor Tom. But he couldn't talk about it without talking about it, and that was more than just a small problem. He was going to have to hearken back to long-forgotten Sunday School lessons that were probably not all that accurate to begin with.

FLIRTATION IN THE KITCHEN

Beauty is power; a smile is its sword.
CHARLES READE

Savannah hovered over the stove like a watchful shepherdess standing over a meadow full of sheep and lambs. Only in this case the sheep were little brown sausages, and somehow happy about it—crisped black in places, just the way her mother had cooked them years ago, and just the way her father had used to praise so ardently.

She then moved swiftly to the right, where the flapjacks had started to have those small little air bubbles break the surface. Savannah flipped them all with a trained hand, and waited a few moments, turning the sausages in order to have something to do.

She filled the platter with the pancakes a moment later, sausages on the side, and handed it without speaking to Mrs. Fuller. That worthy woman was waiting on the table in the dining room, filled with the men making up the search party. Mrs. Fuller was back in short order with an empty platter and set it by the pan, which Savannah had already filled with a new cohort of sausages.

She then turned earnestly to the task of pouring out the batter for the next round of pancakes, and was startled when Mrs. Fuller leaned in and said, "Let me ask just one question, dearie. You do realize you are flirting with him, don't you?"

Savannah swiveled around, genuinely startled. "Flirting? I have been in here virtually the entire time." Pastor Thomas was part of the search party and was one of the men sitting at the table out in the next room. It was five a.m., and Mrs. Fuller had told Sheriff Barnes that he could rendezvous with his party here, get a hearty breakfast, and make their way out to Todd Martin's favorite haunts. Martin had been missing for three days now, and nobody knew if he had been gone a day or two before that.

"Well, dearie, I have only cooked with your kind of intensity two times in my life, and both times there was a man in the other room."

"I do not know to what you could be referring." Savannah tossed her head lightly.

"Do you know why people say that the way to a man's heart is through his stomach? It is a truism, which means that sometimes there is a truth at the bottom of it. There is something to it. That's the thing about truisms. They are often true. And even when they aren't true, some women think they are and act on the basis of it. Either way."

Savannah laughed, but suddenly it sounded a little hollow to her. Mrs. Fuller saw that uncertainty and pressed her point.

"Now I just saw Pastor Thomas's face when he took several of those pancakes of yours—which are fluffy and delightful, by the way—and so I know what he looked like. I have a very simple question for you. Did you imagine what his face looked like when he helped himself to your most delightful breakfast? When he had his first bite?"

The question struck home. She *had* imagined his face as he ate her pancakes, and as he had gazed with admiration upon the sausages. She had imagined it about twenty times.

"Oh, Mrs. Fuller," she said. "I thought you were going to help me."

"I am helping you, as much as you will allow. In here flirting your head off."

Savannah flushed red, and brushed back a lock of hair from her forehead with the back of her hand.

"See, that's another thing you do, you beautiful girl. You have wiles down in your bones. You have ways you know nothing of. It was only a pity that he wasn't in here to see that lovely gesture, brushing back your lovely hair with your lovely hand."

They were talking quietly, which was fortunate, because Pastor Tom was in kitchen, and he had seen it.

"Excuse me," he said. Savannah jumped and stifled a scream.

He looked extremely apologetic. "Excuse me," he said again. "I didn't mean to startle you. I just wanted to thank you both for breakfast. Breakfast was wonderful. I have never seen breakfast done better. We are heading out now. Thanks very much."

He stepped back out of the kitchen, and let the swinging door bump him gently on his shoulder. That gesture . . . the way she just carelessly pushed that hair away from her forehead. And her hair—auburn hair, beautiful hair . . . oh, what's the use right now?

The mountains—not counting the solitary mountain just outside of town—began in earnest about ten miles east of Paradise. Martin himself lived a few miles out of town in that direction already. Three of the men in the search party had hunted with Todd Martin fairly frequently and knew his favorite spots. The three of them split up at the small lake to make their way to those spots, each of them taking one of the other men with him. That left four men. Two of the others were native to the area but had not known Martin. The sheriff sent them north up to the ridge of the mountain and told them to work their way west.

"Pastor Thomas," the sheriff said, "you're new to the area so you can stick with me. Don't want to add to our troubles by getting you lost."

The sheriff and the pastor rode slowly to the southeast. "There's a valley up here that bends to the right," the Sheriff Barnes said. "We will follow the creek at the bottom of it, and then head due east up onto that ridge. Thomason says they hunted up there last fall. I've been there myself a time or two."

Pastor Thomas nodded. As they rode silently, his thoughts drifted back to the surprise visit that Martin had paid him the night before he disappeared. Thomas had told the sheriff that he had seen Martin that night, but hadn't said anything about what they had talked about. "Bible questions," was all he'd said. The sheriff hadn't commented, but he'd filed that away. He didn't take Martin for the kind who would go in for Bible questions.

He had even ventured a comment along those lines. "I never took Martin for a guy with much interest in such things."

"Neither had I," Thomas replied. "Never saw him in church. But his questions were intelligent and went right to the heart of the real issues. It seems to me that something stirred him up though."

Martin had actually awakened him, tapping insistently but quietly on the front door. Pastor Thomas had appeared at the door, his black hair tousled. He had glanced at his pocket watch just before opening the door. Midnight.

He opened the door cautiously, but with a good deal of interest. His eyebrows went up when he saw Todd Martin there. "Todd," he said.

"Pastor Goforth," Martin said. "We met a few weeks back on the trip to Spokane. I thought you would probably remember me."

Thomas gestured him in. "What can I do for you?"

Martin remained on the threshold. "Begging you pardon, reverend. I don't rightly know my p's and q's about all this. I am not a member of your church or any other that I know of. I don't know if I am allowed to ask you questions or not. I am not a sheep from your fold, if you know what I mean. I don't even know if I am a sheep—more of a coyote, maybe. Maybe you should run me off."

Thomas grinned, and gestured again. "Come on in."

Martin nodded gratefully, and came in, holding his hat in both his hands. He went slowly to the couch, and sat down uneasily on the edge of it. Pastor Thomas sat down across from him, looked steadily at him, and said, "How can I help?"

"Well, I think I know that you can help, but I don't rightly know how you might. Here's the situation. I think that I need to be ready to die. I am not afraid of the part before that—I have been in a few scrapes, enough to know that my animal courage is decent enough. What I mean is that while I am not scared of dying, it has recently been borne in on me that I am not ready to die. And I think I ought to be. And that means that maybe I *ought* to be a bit more scared of it."

Pastor Thomas sat quiet for a minute. "I would be happy to talk to you about all of that. But first . . . may I ask why you are asking? Has a doctor told you that you are going to die? Do you have a premonition of it? Dreams?"

"I don't mind you asking, and it certainly would be a natural thing to ask. But I can't rightly talk about that. The story is way too complicated without the whole thing, and there are parts of it that I really can't talk about."

Thomas nodded slightly, as if to say that he respected that. Martin was looking at him expectantly. "Did I make my question clear enough?" he asked.

"Perfectly," Thomas said, and started to clear his throat the way he sometimes did before a sermon. Then he stopped. This wasn't a sermon. "Perfectly," he said again, leaving his throat the way it was. "In order to deal with the problem of how to be ready to die, we have to ask what it is that makes us unready or unprepared. If we are going on a physical journey, the unreadiness would be seen in things like tickets not purchased or suitcases not packed. But what is it that is being left undone when an unready traveler approaches death?"

"That's it exactly," Martin said. He wished he had struck up a friendship with this man instead of with Lambeth.

"The thing that renders us unready to go is sin. The traveler who is not ready is a traveler who does not know what to do with his sin. This is because sin, at bottom, is a refusal to go where we are summoned, and this results in us winding up somewhere else. Another word for that would be lost."

"What is sin? And I don't mean a list of them—I think I understand that. But *what* is it?"

"Sin is being unlike God. Holiness is being like Him. And if someone has persevered in sin, in that attitude of being unlike God, when it comes time to go to meet Him, that person is entirely unready, and there is nothing in the meeting but antipathy. The intent behind bringing us to meet God is so that we might become completely and fully like Him. If we have been spending our time down here going in the other direction, then we are not ready. Some just drift and wander in that direction. Others go industriously in the wrong direction. As one Puritan put it, they sin till they're out of breath."

"What happens to those who meet Him when they are 'not ready'?" Martin asked.

"Can I throw something else into all this first?"

"Certainly," Martin replied.

"When I say Heaven, I am not referring to the kind of sky palace that a superstitious peasant might believe in. And when I refer to Hell, I am not talking about a medieval torture chamber. But they are still real places for all that, and people really do go there. Why I am making this qualification should become obvious in a minute."

Martin nodded. "Go on."

"Heaven can be defined as the presence of God—as much of the presence of the infinite God that finite creatures could take. Hell is defined in Scripture as a place that is *away* from the presence of the Lord. Now this Hell is hellish. It *is* the outer darkness. But for the person who is not ready for Heaven, Heaven would be a worse Hell for him than the actual Hell is. It would be like having your eyes adjusted to a subterranean cavern, and then being taken out into the midday heat and being forced to look directly at the sun. You are not ready."

"Go on," Martin said again.

"The problem with much thinking about Hell, and to a lesser extent Heaven, is that people want to define it all in terms of nerve endings, pleasure and pain. But the universe is a personal place. Heaven is a function of relationship, and Hell is the function of absence of relationship. And because the ruptured relationship between God and man cannot function in a place totally governed by relationship to Him, the only alternative is to be away from Him. But those who are banished are banished by the Lord, from the presence of the Lord, because they will not be done with their case of the everlasting sulks."

"So then, if I feel entirely unready, and I have come to the conviction that I am not making it up . . ." Martin trailed off.

Pastor Thomas leaned forward in his chair. "I think how you framed this whole question in terms of readiness was quite fortunate. Just the other day I was reading from a gentleman over there of the name of Shedd"—here Thomas pointed to his shelves—"and he said that the problem of an unconverted man is that he has an immortal soul and 'that he is utterly unfit and unprepared for such an endless existence.'"

"So how . . ."

"The only way to prepare to meet God there, which is a necessity that none of us can escape, is to go ahead and meet Him here, now. We are not ready in either case, but we can be made ready now."

"And how is that to be done?"

"Well, you knew that you were coming to a Christian pastor. Not surprisingly, the answer to that question is Jesus. But there is a reason for that. Shall I explain it?"

"Please," Martin said. "I am the one who got you out of bed to answer my questions in the middle of the night. I can't complain if you do."

"Our lack of readiness to meet God is an unreadiness that is spread across the entire human race. All of us are not ready. At the beginning of our history, our first father fell away from God, and he represented us fully in that rebellion. Thus we were all of us conceived in rebel territory, if you want to think of it that way. Adam sinned, and in him we all sinned. He sinned representatively. An Adam got us into this fix, and so it would take another Adam to get us out."

"Go on."

"Jesus, the Son of God who became man, is that next Adam. He offers Himself to God as the new and restored humanity, and He offers Himself to us as the way we might approach God as part of that new humanity—instead of as part of the old, damaged humanity."

"How does the death of Jesus enter into it? The cross is central to all of it—it is on top of all the steeples, at any rate. I know that much, but I don't know why."

The two men talked into the night, for at least another hour. At the end of that time Martin said that he had quite enough to think about, and that if he had opportunity, he would come back and resume the conversation. "But now I feel more curious than unready. Thank you."

The two men shook hands, Thomas held open the door, and Todd Martin walked out into the night.

Recalling their parting, Pastor Thomas shook his head to clear it, and pulled himself back to their search. For no reason he could remember later, he rode off the path to make his way over to the lip of a rough slope that tumbled down into a gully with a creek at the bottom. There at the bottom of the gully, on the far side of the creek, a body was sprawled on its back, spread-eagled.

The sheriff had followed Thomas over, and they both said "Martin" at the same moment. The sheriff had recognized his replacement hat, off to the side of the body, while Thomas had recognized his checked waistcoat. He had been wearing that when he was in his study just a few nights before.

The slope was too steep for their horses, so they tethered them to a nearby tree and scrambled down the slope. Thomas felt like one of the stones from the brook had somehow made it into his stomach, one of the rounded ones the size of a couple of fists. He had never seen a dead man before, still less a man dead from a gunshot wound. He did not know why he assumed it would be a gunshot, but he was right. Martin had been shot pointblank in the chest, just once.

Pastor Thomas knelt down beside the body, bowed his head, and said a brief prayer. The sheriff stood back at a respectful distance. First things first. After a moment Thomas opened his eyes, remained kneeling for a few moments more, and then got slowly up.

The murder weapon was lying beside him, as if it had been carelessly thrown there. The sheriff pulled out a handkerchief and picked it up by the barrel, careful not to smudge any fingerprints that might be there. He was quite sure there would be none, but he was careful just the same. He looked at the grip quickly, and there, wood burned into the handle was the name Martin, small but clearly legible. "Shot with his own gun," the sheriff said morbidly. He emptied the chambers, noted that there were five bullets left, wrapped the whole thing up in his handkerchief, and stored it carefully in his pack. The bullets went in a pouch pocket on his vest.

He turned suddenly to Pastor Thomas. "I will walk the area, looking for any clues," he said. "Not that I expect to find anything. You ride down to where the creek meets the road, where that little bridge is. We have not been riding too long. Fire three shots into the air, rapid succession, just like we agreed. The others should hear it and come. They have a stretcher and a blanket, which we will need."

Thomas nodded, and headed back up the slope. On the way back to the bridge, his head was buzzing. He knew that Martin had been preparing to get prepared for death, and he knew that he had shared rudimentary gospel truth with him. He thought briefly, and gratefully, over what he had said. He had some reason for good hope, but he wished he had something more substantial. He was going to have to preach the funeral, he had no doubt, and he had always had a distaste for funerals that simply wished the deceased into Heaven, no matter now dissolute they may have been. And, make no mistake, Martin had been a loose liver, and the whole town knew it.

His three rifle shots summoned the rest of the search party back to where he was waiting for them. It took about forty-five minutes for them all to arrive, and during that time it also summoned a curious old woman who lived out that way. "Just seeing if you were all right," she said, and disappeared again. "Didn't sound like you were shooting at no critter," she said over her shoulder.

As the other men arrived, Pastor Thomas told them that they had found Martin, dead, and that they needed the stretcher and blanket. The men discussed the division of labor briefly, and it was decided that Thomas should be the one who rode back into town to tell the coroner to get ready. When Thomas had once explained where they had found Martin, the others knew immediately where it was.

Thomas rode briskly, sorrowing for Martin, and rolling everything over in his mind. When he got to town he had some trouble finding the coroner, who was down the street from his medical offices telling fishing stories to some friends. But he finally found him and delivered the message, which sent the coroner scurrying.

Pastor Thomas stood on the street outside the saloon where he had found the coroner and thought for a moment. Should he go back to his study first, or should he pick up the mail? It sometimes wasn't delivered this early, but he finally decided to make his way over to the new post office and check.

The mail had been delivered, and there, on the top of a small stack of letters, was a plain envelope, hand-addressed, and no return address. Thomas tore it open, curious, and glanced at the signature. It was a letter from Martin.

AFTERMATH

One half of the world cannot understand
the pleasures of the other.
JANE AUSTEN, *EMMA*

The news of Martin's murder had caused a stir in the town, in part because it was so flagrant and cold-blooded, in part because Martin had been such an affable character around town, in part because it was a small town with not much else to talk about, and in part because this was inexplicable, a true mystery. No one had any ideas about who could have done it or who would have any motivation to do something like that.

Except for Savannah. She knew exactly who had done it, and she knew exactly why. At the same time, her heart was in a perfect commotion. She had never before experienced such a flurry of conflicting emotions. She absolutely needed to talk, and she had no one to talk to. Her primary emotion was one of gratitude to Martin, who had clearly chosen to die rather than reveal her secret. She did not know what his motivation for that could possibly have been, but she was simply grateful to him. It was a sacrifice she never would have asked him to make, but he had made it, willingly, on his own. And he had done that with nothing in his past to indicate that he might have the capacity to be so . . . *noble*. After his death, a few stories floated by her that she couldn't help overhearing, and while he seemed like a friendly enough fellow, he had haunted saloons, lost a goodish bit of money at cards, spent plenty of time in some suspect areas of nearby towns, places where the ladies wore their make-up thick and their morals thin, and other similar whispers. All in all, his sacrifice for her had simply seemed to come out of nowhere.

This was nobility and courage *ex nihilo*. Savannah knew that it had to have come from somewhere, but it was certainly inexplicable on the surface.

Savannah's second emotion, a distant second to the first, was relief that the one person who knew her secret was dead. She reacted to herself furiously whenever she felt that emotion starting to take shape, but she *did* feel it taking shape at different times, and was very distraught with herself—distraught with herself and ashamed. A time or two she got into a fierce argument with herself over it—she somehow felt that she should be grateful for his sacrifice, but that it would be ignoble to enjoy the fruit of that sacrifice. That was another reason she felt like she needed to talk with someone, anyone wise.

The third problem had to do with what she needed to do. This is where the real dilemma was. What was her moral duty in this? A murder had been committed, and she knew the identity of the killer. But the only way she could talk about it would be by telling the sheriff about her early morning conversation with Martin. But she couldn't do that without revealing what the conversation was about. If she did that, then Lambeth would just deny everything, and she couldn't prove any element of it. She had no proof, nothing. It would be her word against Lambeth's, and the only thing that would make it noteworthy would be the scandalous element concerning herself. And that, if she were foolish enough to do it, would turn Martin's death into a vain gesture—because he had died to keep secret what she would then reveal after the fact. The only advantage would be the slight possibility that Lambeth might be charged, or that something new might come out as a result of her confessing. At the same time, it did not seem right to say nothing. She couldn't say nothing, and she couldn't say anything. She needed to talk with someone, and could not talk with anyone.

Her dilemma would have been even more acute if she had known that Lambeth knew that Martin had talked to her. She did not know that *she* was in any danger at all. She knew that Lambeth had gotten the word *Milwaukee* from Martin, and that was all. He had tried to bluff her into giving herself away, but that had not happened. She did not know that Lambeth had seen Martin in the alley behind her house. And while she knew that Lambeth was a very bad man—and she knew now he was capable of murder—she did not know how bent and broken he was.

She also suspected he had had something to do with the fire, but she couldn't fit that piece in anywhere. It was too random, and didn't make sense.

What about Pastor Thomas? Why couldn't she talk to him? He was her pastor, after all. She knew she could trust his counsel, but he was the one person she feared talking to the most. He could tell her what to do, he could give her godly counsel, but he couldn't tell her anything—if she told him everything—without never wanting to see her again. She could feel his condemnation already, and thought she would die if he reacted that way. How could he not react that way, such a gifted minister? She knew he was a good man, and that he would not condemn her openly, but that did not change the force of the emotion. He would condemn her in his heart, somewhere down in his heart. How could he not?

She needed to talk with someone. She couldn't talk with Mrs. Fuller because that would simply plunge Mrs. Fuller into the same dilemma.

Savannah spent two sleepless nights this way, and decided at four a.m. the second night that she would seek out Pastor Thomas, and tell him two-thirds of her story. She would tell him that she knew who had murdered Martin, and that she knew because Martin had spoken to her about how Lambeth was interested in getting certain information out of him . . . could she just stop there? Suppose Pastor Thomas looked at her with that way that he had, and he told her that she had to tell him everything? What would she do then?

What if he asked what the "certain information" was? What *that* was, she could always say, she was not prepared to go into at the present time. But another glaring problem stood out. Why would Martin confide anything to Savannah? They had only met once on that trip to Spokane. Why would he tell her anything of great importance? Pastor Thomas was no fool. He would guess instantly that Martin had told Savannah something because it had concerned Savannah.

She made her decision to do something by Saturday morning, and thought that she could commit herself after church to Pastor Thomas by asking for an appointment the next day. Then she would be all in, couldn't change her mind, and that part would be all settled.

The time until Sunday morning went by so slowly that it ached, and after she spoke with him about meeting the next day, *that* time flew by so quickly there were a few moments she thought she felt the breeze in her hair. Pastor Thomas had been mysteriously standing alone after church, which was not usually the case, so Savannah approached him quickly, quietly, and

asked if she could please see him the following morning. Was his schedule free? Yes, it was. That would be
no problem. He would be happy to.

Monday morning was upon her almost right away.
She stood outside his parsonage, swallowing hard, not
knowing if she could do it. She finally thought that she
had to do what she had to do, gave herself a fierce little
command, which was to simply take one step toward
his door, and trust that the events of her day would
sweep her into the rest of the necessary steps. She found
herself at the door, and she politely knocked on it.

Pastor Thomas called her in, and was halfway to
the door when she came in. He invited her to take a
seat, and when they were both seated, he began by astonishing her beyond all measure.

He said, "I know that you want to ask me about
something, or tell me something, but if you don't
mind, I would like to go first."

Savannah blinked, startled. After a second, she
said, "Well, yes, of course."

Thomas nodded. "When I am finished, you can
tell me what you came to tell me, if you still feel like
you need to. It is *possible* that you might no longer feel
it necessary."

Savannah sat motionless, not sure what kind of
expression was on her face. She hoped it was intelligent. She nodded her head. "Go on," she managed to
say softly.

"Given what I know, I was wondering if you were
going to talk to me. If I didn't hear from you in the next

day or so, I was going to ask you if I could see you. But I am very pleased you have come. It shows, in my view, a very high degree of character. Your visit here concerns the death of Todd Martin, does it not?"

Savannah nodded her head again, mystified.

Pastor Thomas resumed. "I should start at the beginning. Todd Martin had once been friends with Alan Lambeth, and for some reason they had a falling out, but which no one knew about. That happened just a few weeks ago. As a result of that falling out, there was some kind of threat that Lambeth directed at Martin. At the same time, for reasons that were possibly related to all of this, Martin went through some sort of spiritual awakening. Because of his questions he had related to all of that, he came to see me seeking answers. In the course of our discussion, I learned what I have just told you. I also learned from Martin that you had something to do with their falling out. Martin didn't tell me what it was, but I knew that your name was involved in it. Given the fact that Lambeth had once been sweet on you, which the whole town knows, and had experienced your fury at the picnic, various possible scenarios presented themselves to me. All of this meant that there was some kind of possible motive for Martin's death. I have taken the liberty of speaking to Sheriff Barnes about what I know, and he is fully aware of all the possibilities in this. He is taking these possibilities into his account. There is no need for me to speak with him further, or for you to speak with him at all, if you were feeling that you might have a duty to do so."

Savannah sat, stupefied. Pastor Thomas appeared to do nothing whenever he was around her but create conflicting emotions in her. At this moment she felt a tangled combination of angry, relieved, patronized, protected, loved, and insulted. She did not trust herself to speak. She had no idea at all what would come out if she tried to speak. She just sat. After a moment she licked her lips. Then she sat a little more. She still did not trust herself to talk.

Pastor Thomas was way out in front of her, far down the road. He had solved all of her problems. She was profoundly grateful. He had done it without consulting her, or checking with her, or anything like that. He had just *gone* to the sheriff. She felt patronized. She also felt like he was protecting her. That made her feel warm. She felt foolish. That made her angry.

She decided to mortify most of the emotions that were churning around inside her and spoke politely, not icily, as she stood to go. "Pastor Thomas, you appear to have anticipated all my concerns. I thank you greatly for your zeal for my welfare, and for taking care of everything so . . . *handily.*" She hoped that this last word didn't sound tart.

But by the time she got to the door, she decided that it hadn't sounded tart enough at all, and that she very much wanted to say something that sounded just a little bit astringent. He couldn't just come in and take her under his wing, without so much as a by-your-leave, and then have her just go along with him meekly. This was far worse than the time he had rescued her at the

Davenport. She had submitted meekly then, but only because Mr. Watkins was impossible to deal with. She was going to let him know now that there was some fire in her. She was not some china doll that he could put on the shelf just where he wanted her in order to be able to see and admire. She ought to have been *consulted*.

When she got to the door, she turned back. "Pastor Thomas, your attentions on my behalf have in fact solved a number of problems, some of which were in fact keeping me up nights. But for you to go to the sheriff and talk to him about Martin, without mentioning anything about it to me, although it concerns me greatly, seems to me to have been more than a little bit *proud*." She accented the last word heavily.

With that, his eyebrows went up. "Proud?"

"Yes, proud." Savannah remembered a book she had read years before when she was a little girl in which the heroine had tossed her curls. She thought of doing that now, but didn't do anything. But the way she stood there at the doorway looked as though she just *had* tossed them.

Pastor Thomas got up and walked toward her slowly. "Well, I am very sorry that I have given offense in any way. That was not my intent. And I acknowledge that I am a sinner, and that pride is always right in the middle of everything. But pride had nothing to do with me going to the sheriff. I had the same dilemma in my conscience that you appear to have had. Martin came to me independently with some spiritual questions, and I had very good reason to believe that his visit was related to the person who murdered him. And I believed that I knew something the sheriff needed to know. So I don't believe pride was involved in that part at all."

"*That* part?" Savannah continued to look very serious. But Thomas was having trouble noticing how serious she was being because all his attention was fully occupied in noticing how beautiful she was being.

"Yes. I do confess," he said, coming a step closer, "that pride, or perhaps some sort of vainglory, had something to do with how I spoke to *you* about it just now. May I tell you the reason?"

"No!" Savannah said, without thinking.

"You have charged me with the sin of pride," he said. "Why may I not confess to you why I think there may be *some* element of truth to your charge?"

Savannah did not know what he was about to say, but she was most definitely aware of the fact that her rebuke of him as she was preparing to leave had gotten away from her, and that he was now somehow back in control of the situation. She also had a definite sense that here was a man on the verge of declaring himself, declaring his affections. She had been in this situation before, and she could tell that in this one respect, he was not departing from the playbook that all men apparently had.

"No," she said again, nervously. "I don't think it would be appropriate. Whatever it is."

He took another step closer. "I do think there is something about what I would say that could give you something to think about. And if I have wronged you by my vainglory, I would like a chance to put it right."

"No, no," she said hurriedly. "There is nothing that you need to put right. I ought not to have questioned your motives. I don't know you well enough to intrude in that way, and I really must be going. I *must*."

Thomas saw that she was intent on doing so, and so he stepped quickly to the side and opened the door. He bowed slightly. "Although you forbade me to speak to you about it, I will carefully consider what you have said. And perhaps we can speak about it at some other time."

The door closed behind her, and Savannah stood on the front step for a moment collecting her breath, her thoughts, and her wits. How had he *done* that? Every time she sought to get a step ahead of him, he was already there. She liked it very much. It annoyed her very much.

As the door closed, Pastor Thomas stood quietly inside the door, with his hand on the handle. For a moment he thought he should open the door up, pursue her down the walk, and just take her in his arms. *That* would excite some comment. She would probably scream and slap him.

Savannah stood quietly outside the door, on the front porch. She was speaking to herself furiously under her breath. Why do I *do* that? I was going to leave without saying anything, and then I turn around at the door and just give him an opening. She stood, hesitating, thinking that she should turn around and tap on the door, and briefly apologize. And if he took her in his arms, she would just have to deal with it.

Thomas stood inside the door, eyes on the floor. He put his right hand up and rested it on the door. He was thinking hard. He knew he was going to talk with her openly. Should it be today? There was still time.

Savannah had turned around and was facing the door. Not knowing why, she reached up and touched the door with her left hand, gently, just with her fingers. Should she knock?

Thomas shook his head, hoping to clear it. He knew that she knew he was attracted to her. He knew, or thought he knew, why she was reluctant, and that it had something to do with her past. He thought that her problem was not with *him*, although he wasn't entirely sure of that. His pastoral sense took over, and he told himself that talking to her today would be forcing it. He should make sure he was not being impatient. Whenever he was around her, it was frightfully easy to be impatient.

Savannah shook her head. *Impossible.* It was just impossible, regardless of how she felt about it. She might feel very sad about it, and most certainly would feel sad about it. But that wouldn't make it any less impossible. She sighed.

They both turned away from the door at the same moment, neither of them knowing that a spell had been broken.

And the farther from the door each of them got, the more impossible a relationship between the two of them seemed to each of them. Savannah held to the impossibility of the relationship as an intellectual constant, although her emotions fluctuated wildly. She knew it was impossible, and desperately felt like it might not be on various occasions. Thomas was in an opposite condition. His emotional state was fixed, and he knew that he loved her. And intellectually he was confident also—whenever he was with her. That is what projected the fixed certainty that she could feel as a palpable presence. But when he was away from her, when he was left alone with his own thoughts, his intellectual confidence that he would eventually win her would evaporate like dew off a melon in August.

And so it was that Thomas sat down behind his desk, ran his fingers through his hair, and quietly despaired.

THE NEXT STEP
DOWN

Of all the seven deadly sins, only Envy is no fun at all.
JOSEPH EPSTEIN

By the time Lambeth had come to shoot Martin, it was hardly a remarkable step for him. It was a small step, and it was simply the *next* step. But the first big step had occurred when he was mostly still a boy— and that had been the momentous turn. Everything after that moment had come simply in small increments, according to their appointed and necessary schedule.

He had once been with some five other young men, sometime in early autumn, out by a creek back

131

in Delaware, where he was originally from. A large flat meadow lay on one side of the creek, and the boys were pitting themselves against one another in various feats of speed and strength, the way that young men love to do. They were throwing large rocks to see who could hit the trees furthest away across the creek. They were racing along one particularly level stretch by the creek. One of them had seen a picture of some Highland games and the caber toss. They had found an old railroad tie and had been trying to throw that.

During all such events, Alan Lambeth consistently dominated. He had actually selected his acquaintances with just such a result in view—although he had not stated it to himself that way with any degree of clarity. He had always been intensely competitive, and he always hated losing, and so he had naturally gravitated to a circle of friends among whom he could win, and who would naturally defer to him. And this the boys dutifully did, almost always.

All was going the way it usually did when another young man, a cousin of one of the regulars, showed up, apparently uninvited. It came out later that his cousin had actually urged him to come, but this took a while to find out because Lambeth was so angry about what had happened. The reason he became so angry was that the new arrival, whose name was Jake, insufferable Jake, intolerable Jake, was everything that Lambeth was not. He was tall, he was affable, he was easygoing, he was good-looking, obviously intelligent, and naturally athletic. He had probably not trained a

day in his life, and yet he was simply good at everything. Lambeth trained daily, intensely, every morning with a medicine ball, and was good at every skill
he managed to chase down. But he had to chase them
all down, and pin each one. He labored for all of it, as
though hounds were on his trail.

Every game the boys had set up that afternoon,
Jake simply excelled in and laughed heartily in the
course of it. Once, while throwing rocks across the
creek, he had slipped and fallen, and he laughed
heartily at *that*. He thought it was the most wonderful
thing that had happened to him in a month. In short,
he arrived and started beating everyone at virtually
everything while simultaneously not caring if he won
at anything at all. Lambeth had never met such mas-
culine ease, and he hated it. He loathed it, and did not
know why he loathed it. He knew instinctively that
if Jake beat him, it would matter to him and not at all
to Jake, and that if he ever beat Jake at anything, it
wouldn't matter to Jake and would consequently be
worthless to him.

The decisive moment, the turn, came on the way
home that evening, when Lambeth, still seething from
his humiliations, decided that he would forever hate
what he naturally wanted to hate. He declared war
on it. An unknown enmity had him by the throat,
and would not let him go. The humiliation descended
upon him, and Lambeth invited it in to stay. From that
moment on he decided to use it as an additional spur
in everything he did.

And so it was, from that day on, that he overcame every obstacle that came into his path, not without effort, but rather handily. Fortunately for his comparative peace of mind, he had never again met anyone like that detestable Jake character . . . until Pastor Thomas. That moment some months before when Savannah had seen them warily greeting each other at the church door was the moment that Lambeth knew that he was in the presence of another one just like Jake, the same ease, the same confidence, the same standing, living, breathing, *insult.*

One difference was that Jake was young enough to be oblivious to the effect he was having, while Thomas had been around long enough to know something about Lambeth's reactions to him. He saw Lambeth as a threat immediately, and knew, almost as immediately, that the issue was envy. Thomas did not acknowledge this to himself in a manner that flattered himself—many good men do not suspect the course of the antipathy directed at them because they are too humble to think they might be the object of anything like envy. Thomas knew what it was, but construed it as something inside Lambeth that had been operating on him long before Thomas had moved to Paradise. Thomas knew that envy is usually an internally driven thing, and so the object of the envy need not start taking any bows. And so it was that Thomas didn't take any bows, which just made the problem worse.

Thomas was comfortable with who he was. He delighted when others surpassed him, and he accepted it with gratitude when he surpassed others. He had graduated from seminary with high honors, and had accomplished this by means of hard work, hard work that he was able to hold up to God with an open palm. If God accepted it, He accepted it. If He did not, then it was already surrendered.

The other issue for Lambeth was Savannah. She was the first goal, the first trophy, the first "first place finish," that had ever been denied him. Everything else that he had ever *determined* to get, he had eventually gotten. He was first in his class graduating from the university. He was the youngest bank president in his company west of the Mississippi. He was the wealthiest man in Paradise. He had golden ambitions. He already had his eye on the governor's mansion, and why not? And all of it seemed worthless to him now because Savannah had simply *rejected* him. Out of hand. Not only so, but then she had humiliated him at the park. He had to be in control, and he was not in control of her in any way. She had become intolerable to him.

When he had thrown the word *Milwaukee* at her, he was self-consciously running a bluff. He knew the bluff might not work, meaning that he might not get the information he wanted. But the failure of his bluff, the *way* it failed, rankled him also. She had just stood there, serene and untouched. Her unflappable response made him doubt, more than once, whether Martin really knew anything about what he was talking about. But the way Martin died indicated that

Martin, at least, thought that Milwaukee was highly significant. And he had seen him coming out into that alley behind Savannah's boardinghouse. *That* had to mean something. But at the most, it meant that Martin *thought* he knew something. Maybe the nice woman dismissed that unfortunate man for coming around to her place early in the morning to talk nonsense at her. Lambeth found himself worried again. Maybe there really was nothing.

But whether there was nothing or not, Savannah had stood there unruffled, listening to his dark hints, *acting* as if it were nothing. Acting as if *he* were nothing, and *that* was the intolerable thing. She had shown no awareness of his strength. She had acted as though she did not care what he knew. Arrogant, insolent, self-righteous . . . Lambeth checked himself. He had no moral problem with invective, but he knew that he would not be any farther along if he spent too much energy on it.

All of this was bad, but the worst was the fact that he saw, more clearly than anyone else in the town, that Savannah looked up to and respected Pastor Thomas Goforth. He saw it more clearly than she did. He could feel the muscle over his left cheekbone twitching. And all that man had done was ride the train into town to start preaching *sermons*. Lambeth's lip curled. He licked his teeth, and could taste the disdain. That first sermon had been a disaster—how anybody could respect a babbler like that was beyond him. He grudgingly acknowledged that the sermons after that were not in the same category, but even the good ones were just *talking*.

He had several times caught Savannah looking at Thomas with what could only be interpreted as admiration. And he had gone to her repeatedly, hat in hand, and she just refused. She rebuffed him. She had never looked at him that way, and he worked more than anyone he had ever met. And Thomas had arrived in town, and had done nothing, and she admired him. It was obvious. If Lambeth had known the meaning of the word *grace*, he would have applied it here. But he did not know it, and that was the heart of the problem actually.

Up to this point, he had been dimly aware of Elizabeth Sarandon, that pretty girl who lived in the same boardinghouse as did Savannah. Now rejected by Savannah, goaded by Thomas, and provoked by Martin, he knew that he needed to approach the situation with more resources. He thought that this Elizabeth had noticed him, and had been trying to get his attention. He would find out soon enough if that were the case. And he also thought he had noticed a promising disdain for Savannah in her.

After asking a few tellers at the bank, he found out that Elizabeth worked at David's, the department store at the center of town. No time like the present, he thought, and walked over to the store shortly before noon. He walked around the store briefly until he saw her—she was working in the millinery section. She walked over in surprise. "Mr. Lambeth!" she said.

"I am very sorry to disturb you at work," he said. "But I thought that we probably ought to get better acquainted. I have been meaning to ask you for some time," he lied, "but I decided to get around to it today. Would you be free if I were to ask you to dinner this evening?"

Elizabeth blushed slightly. She had not been expecting this at all, and was almost entirely unprepared. "Where?" she said. It was a foolish question, because there was only one restaurant in town, the one right across the street at the main hotel. There were a few hash-slinging places, but they only served breakfast and lunch for the workmen.

"I was thinking here in town," Lambeth said. He nodded toward the direction of the street. "At the hotel."

"I would be pleased and flattered," Elizabeth said.

Lambeth actually knew how to be charming if he had a willing audience. If anybody was watching who knew what actual charm was, the effect was totally other than charming, but whenever someone *wanted* to be charmed—as Elizabeth most certainly did—he knew how to ladle it out of the pot.

As they sat down at their table just a few hours later, Lambeth decided to take the direct approach. "I must begin with an apology," he said. "That is part of the reason why I needed to ask you to dinner."

"An apology! Mr. Lambeth, I don't see how that could be possible."

"Alan, please," he said. "Call me Alan."

"All right, then, Alan," she said. "I do not see how an apology could possibly be called for."

THE NEXT STEP DOWN

"Well, this is awkward," he said, "but it will not have escaped your notice that last year I sought the attentions of your housemate Savannah?"

Elizabeth's expression clouded. It had not escaped her notice. "Go on," she said.

"She is attractive in her way, and when I happened to meet her after I arrived here in Paradise, she was able to withhold . . . um . . . a more complete picture from me. I frankly admit to having had some level of attraction and curiosity. But after my dealings with her last year, and her recent outburst of temper at the church picnic—which I assume you heard about—I must confess her true character then became manifestly apparent to me."

Elizabeth nodded, enjoying the direction this appeared to be taking. "All of this is obvious to those of us who live with her," she contributed, "but I fail to see how it in any way requires an apology to me."

All of this was a soothing balm on Elizabeth's chafed sensitivities, and Lambeth had chosen his approach well. A certain kind of beauty flourishes when another kind is diminished. At the same time, Elizabeth did have a conscience, and hers started bothering her as soon as she spoke the way she did about Savannah. But the part of her heart that wanted to be flattered was easily louder.

She looked at Lambeth quizzically, but was smart enough not to look coquettish. She looked, in fact, like an educated twentieth-century woman. She did not look at all like a woman who was falling for a line, and that was not because the restaurant lights were dim.

"What many people don't know," Lambeth continued, "is that she not only threw that bowl at me—which could have seriously hurt me had she been a better shot—but before she threw it, when I came up to offer her that potato salad, she whispered a taunt at me that was perhaps the vilest thing I have ever heard a woman say."

In saying this Lambeth had come dangerously close to overplaying his hand, and the only thing that prevented his spell being entirely broken was the fact that Elizabeth was by this point desperately curious to find out what he was going to say about Savannah. But something, somewhere, deep inside her was troubled by him. She had lived with Savannah for years, and though she did not like her, and though she thought she was too pretty by half, and though she thought that someone that beautiful should really have a brain made out of cotton candy, she did know that what Lambeth was saying about Savannah was entirely out of character. Something about Lambeth's lie clanked. Because of her curiosity, the clanking sound was distant, several rooms away, but she did hear it.

"I see," she said, with wonder in her voice. "I won't ask you what she said. But I still don't know how this means you need to apologize to me."

"She is a beauty, I know, but these revelations about her have shown me that hers is a beauty that is truly superficial. I ought to have known better, I should have seen right through it. But I did not . . . and here is where the apology comes . . . had I been paying closer attention to another beauty, one who was right next to her, I would have been spared a lot of grief. And so the apology," Lambeth concluded, "is extended to you because of my failure to have eyes in my head." And here, even though he was seated, he bowed gallantly.

Elizabeth flushed. She was pleased, distressed, gratified, suspicious, and yet still pleased. She had been trying to get Lambeth's attention for many months, and it was gratifying that she now had it. But something sounded hollow. Her pleasure was not yet complete.

Lambeth, for his purposes, was not at all interested in Elizabeth, except as a tool to help him get Savannah out of his head—that and to get back at Savannah. He knew that he had no real way of getting close to Elizabeth except by pretending to court her, and he knew there were plenty of ways he could just walk away when he had whatever he needed. He was not smitten, but he was certainly willing to act like it. And Elizabeth somehow knew he was not smitten, and that he was just acting, and that Savannah would never have said anything vile, and yet here he was, paying close attention to her. She blinked twice, and without even noticing it she made her decision. Her worries fluttered for a moment, the way her parakeet had done once in her hand for a moment. But she just put it back in the cage, and dropped the cloth over the top of it.

When she looked up, her smile was bright and uncluttered. "Mr. Lambeth . . . Alan!" she said. "You are most kind."

"And so forgive my very bad manners," he said, "for bringing our friend up. I felt I needed to do it right at the start so that things would be completely clear between us. I didn't see how I could not do it, and I didn't see how I could do it without a grotesque breach of manners. I hope I have not blundered too badly. But with that unpleasant task done . . . tell me about yourself. How did you first come to Paradise?"

Her story was similar to many who lived in Paradise. There were very few natives, just a handful of women from the pioneer times. They had lived here since they were girls, the three ladies on the south side. But Elizabeth had come out three years before in search of . . . she wasn't sure of what, exactly, and she hadn't found it yet. But she had found Paradise a very pleasant little town—she had dropped in to visit with her cousin who was here—and after staying for a few weeks decided to try for a job, which she immediately got. It was all very acceptable, and she might as well be here as somewhere else. Paradise would do. She smiled invitingly. His turn.

He told his story, the way he had learned to tell it to women. He was filled with boasts, but most of the time he was aware enough of himself that he could keep it in, or work things in obliquely. He knew that people hated it when he was manifestly superior to them—and he largely knew this because of how much he hated it when he had met someone who felt superior to him. He wasn't sure how he knew they felt that way. They just exuded it.

And so he spoke to her of his time in college, his ambitions, his trip west, his job at the bank in Chicago, and how he was offered this post here in Paradise, far ahead of many men in his cohort. He had leapt at the chance, and had been laboring mightily since he got here.

"I have labored almost hard enough"—and here he paused deliberately for just a moment—"to not notice my lack of feminine companionship."

She smiled at this, flushed very slightly, and nodded her receipt of the compliment. She knew it was a line, and a line well-practiced on others, and for some reason that did not matter. Elizabeth was a bright woman, with an active intelligence. It was not that she did not notice what he was doing, or what she was doing in response. She saw it all quite clearly, and then deliberately, carefully, with her eyes open, she just placed another bird in the cage, and lowered the cover again.

The rest of the dinner went smoothly, with both parties engaged, off and on, in acceptable levels of flirtation. A plan was forming in Lambeth's mind, and it was not one that required him to hurry. She was trying to decide what he was up to, and thinking through how likely she was to go along, and was coming to the conclusion that it was pretty likely. He escorted her from the dining area, took her hand leading down the front steps, and then presented his arm to her. "May I walk you home?"

"I would be delighted."

As they approached the boardinghouse, Lambeth looked ahead and saw with grim satisfaction that

Savannah was coming from the other direction. She was farther off from the house than they were, so the couple turned up the front walk before it was necessary to greet her. But they saw her, and she most clearly saw them. *Delightful*, Lambeth thought. I don't have to depend on people inside the boardinghouse gossiping. Just cut out the middle man.

He walked Elizabeth to the door, released her from his arm, bowed and tipped his hat. "May I call on you again?" She nodded with a smile.

Alan Lambeth kept his hat off so that he could motion with it to Savannah as he passed her on the front walk, which he did. As soon as he was past her, he pulled it on to his head with a decided jerk.

The sheriff spun Todd Martin's funny little bowler hat on the desk in front of him, still muttering to himself. He had a murder charge to lodge against somebody, and a manslaughter charge to lodge against somebody. And maybe the dead man was the arsonist, but if not then hopefully the killer and the arsonist would be the same somebody. *That* would cut down on the paperwork.

Martin had been a suspect in the arson/manslaughter case, on the strength of the hat being there at the scene, which was a little too convenient, and on the basis of Lambeth saying that he thought he had seen Martin that night. But Martin's alibi was as ironclad as an alibi can be. One of the men who swore that Martin had been playing cards with him all night long, many miles away, had given the kind of testimony that

Barnes could put in the bank. Barnes had known that witness for years, a man named Cooper, and would trust him with a couple of his lives, if he had that many.

So the next obvious person to wonder about was Lambeth. The night of the fire, he had been trapped in front of his bank with a broken leg. But *when* had he broken his leg? Barnes had visited Dr. Gritman a couple times to ask about that. Wasn't there any way he could determine, or even guess, how long the leg had been broken when Lambeth was first brought in? *Mebbe*, Gritman had said—he didn't talk like an educated doctor—"mebbe I could've if I had been looking for that information at the *time*, but I really wasn't."

He had been thinking of other things with any surplus mental energy he might have had. That night he had delivered one baby, tried and failed to save Mrs. Watson, and had then set Lambeth's leg. "Whenever I had a minute to think, I was thinking about bed. Not about how long Lambeth's leg had been broke."

"Well, thanks for nothing," the sheriff said, getting up to go.

"No need to be snippy, son." Gritman grinned at him. "I wouldn't want to change my mind about wanting to help you out. Why you are asking all this is a little bit transparent to me, although some might still wonder at it. Why would the most successful man in Paradise take it into his noggin to run down the street in the middle of the night to set fire to a boarding-house? That is a question well worth asking. But if you failed to ask it, you might miss out on the fact that the pulchritudinous Miss Westmoreland lives there." He pronounced it *pulchritooodinous*, savoring the word as it came out, treating it like it was a butterscotch lozenge.

"So?" The sheriff asked.

"Well, apparently you need to work on your roster of gossipy informants. Have you ever stopped to think about how much police work depends on gossip? Lambeth tried to court her last year and was turned down flat, flatter than a pancake made with really thin batter. Lambeth took it ill."

"Lambeth takes most everything ill."

"Right. But you *did* hear about the great potato salad throw, didn't you?"

Sheriff Barnes shook his head. It might have been that he was the only person in town who hadn't.

"There is some real bad blood between those two. I heard that Lambeth called her some horrific name, the kind of name my sainted mother never heard of, and she threw a small bowl of potato salad at the back of his head, and I heard that her aim was unerring and true."

The sheriff scratched the back of his head. "But surely Lambeth wouldn't try to murder a whole boardinghouse full of people over something like his wounded vanity. Surely he wouldn't try to murder Miss Savannah over something like that . . . and all those other people with her. As much as I would like to believe the worst about him, surely he can't be all that bad. Or even if he might be that bad, he would scarcely be that stupid."

Gritman smiled at the sheriff again. "Think, my boy. *Think*. If you have Lambeth written down in your notebook as a suspect to any extent at all—and this is just between you and me—you surely don't think that the broken leg was part of his plan? That had to be simple bad luck. So the only thing you need to know is if he was an unlucky criminal or an unlucky bad man who was innocent this time."

"Go on."

"So if he was not *planning* on having a broken leg, he could have used his two good legs to run off to be home in bed after he lit the fire, that's one possibility. That way he doesn't enter into the picture at all."

"Or?"

"Or he was planning on running down to the boardinghouse to be a big hero, rescuing all the people from the fire he just set."

Gritman was a great devourer of mystery and detective stories, and he was enjoying himself immensely. By this point he was leaning back in his chair, and had both feet on his desk. Several times already he had refrained from saying, "Elementary, my dear Barnes."

Barnes objected, shaking his head. "That seems . . . unlikely to me. If Lambeth had called her some vile name, and she had humiliated him yet one *more* time, how could he think he could patch things up with her by showing off? He had to know that wouldn't work."

"I have the advantage on you there. I know Lambeth pretty well from any number of tedious Chamber meetings. He acts the way a peacock would if a peacock had any brains. He is really smart, but a large part of his mental energy is spent constantly looking out the corner of his eye hoping to catch a mirror nearby."

"So . . ."

Gritman interrupted him. "Look. Lambeth wanted to save her, along with everybody else in Mrs. Fuller's house, not so that she would fall into his arms crying 'my hero,' but rather so that she would be irritated into the ground."

The two men sat there quietly for a moment.

Then Gritman added, "He didn't want to rescue her for the sake of her gratitude. He wanted to rescue her for the sake of his revenge."

"Okay," Sheriff Barnes muttered, after a moment. "You got yourself a reasonable hypothesis here."

"Then why so glum? It seems to me that after the sterling help you have received here, you ought to be rubbing your hands together, the way law enforcement officials like to do."

"Well, because I suspect—but do not yet know— that Lambeth will have an alibi, somehow, for the time before the fire, and before his broken leg. When he was going to be the hero, with nobody dead, that wasn't as important. But if he has not come up with a story that covers him good, then I'm a Hottentot. I need to meet with him again, but me hearing an airtight alibi is almost a certainty."

"Aren't you going to ask me about the murder of Todd Martin?"

"No, I wasn't."

"Well, that's fine," Gritman said. "Because I don't have any ideas there. It is a shame because the two things seem like they have to be related, but I don't see how they could be."

Sheriff Barnes was right about the alibi. Or perhaps he was right. He was possibly right. He actually wasn't sure.

He decided to ask Lambeth straight up the middle if he had any way of accounting for his whereabouts in the hours before he broke his leg. "Just trying to cover all the bases here," he said gamely.

Lambeth had been expecting the question, and—as the sheriff had predicted to Gritman—he had the matter covered. "Sorry," he told the sheriff, "but you can't just walk down the street and check on my story. But you *can* check on it."

"So how would I go about doing that?"

Lambeth scribbled an address on an index card with a name scrawled across the top. "This gent is named Peterson. Aaron Peterson. He is the new vice-president of our Portland branch. We are on the eastern edge of his region, and he has been traveling around to all the area banks in order to grasp the extent of his responsibilities. He just wanted to meet all the bank managers, shake their hands, look them in the eye, and generally act the part he thinks he is supposed to act. He came here late that afternoon, right after we closed, and I spent a couple hours with him that evening."

"How long was that?" the sheriff asked.

"From about 6:30 to 8:30. I walked him back to the train station about 8:30, made the mistake of popping back in here for a few minutes to finish up a few things. I worked for maybe another half an hour, then left to go home. And as you know, I snapped my leg outside."

Lambeth had found out from a friend at the fire department when the chief had calculated the start of the fire, and so he backed up his leg break to some hours before that. And he was pretty sure that no one could establish or show that his leg had actually been broken sometime after the fire had started. A broken leg was a broken leg.

And as for Peterson, it was certainly true that he was a new vice-president in Portland. But he was also an old companion of Lambeth's, one who had engaged in more than a few shady deals back east—together with Lambeth—before both of them had decided to try their hand at making their fortune out west. Peterson owed Lambeth at least a couple of lies.

"Write to this address," Lambeth said, "and ask Mr. Peterson where he was on that night, and with whom, and I am sure he will be glad to tell you all about it."

The sheriff had dutifully done so, and Peterson had written back, most courteously, and filled in all the gaps, just as Lambeth had requested. He left himself available for any further inquiries, and remained most eager to be of assistance.

The sheriff muttered to himself, and ran his hands through his hair.

ELIZABETH AND SAVANNAH

Beauty is only skin deep, but ugly goes clean to the bone.
DOROTHY PARKER

When Savannah entered, Elizabeth was already standing on the far side of the living room, hanging up her jacket and gloves. Whenever she wasn't speaking, she was a beautiful woman, and there were times when she could be striking. But whenever she spoke, a look of disdain would cloud her countenance. But she wasn't speaking now, and her long blond hair cascaded down her back. Savannah closed the front door quietly behind her, looked across at Elizabeth and simply admired her.

151

She decided that she wouldn't begin a conversation with Elizabeth about anything important, other
than simply greeting her. If Elizabeth began something, then perhaps. Maybe. But what could she say in
response? She couldn't act excited that Lambeth had
taken Elizabeth out. That was not good news. But she
could not simply be rude. Savannah knew instinctively
that any kind of negative response from her would be
taken as competitive and catty. But any kind of posi-
tive response would be profoundly dishonest and hyp-
ocritical, and it would be the kind of hypocrisy that
Elizabeth would see through instantly.

She needed time to think about it. But could she just
ignore the fact that she had just seen Elizabeth on Lambeth's arm, walking her up to the front door? Under
ordinary circumstances, of course she would have said
something. She corrected herself. She would have said
something if Elizabeth had a beau other than Lambeth.
Lambeth would be a disaster for this poor woman. Savannah had never taken to Elizabeth, but she didn't dis-
like her. And she certainly didn't wish Lambeth on her.

Savannah decided to simply walk past with a
cheerful greeting, in the hope that Elizabeth would say
nothing in return. She almost made it.

The only reason Elizabeth spoke is that she was trying to quiet certain restive voices in her conscience. She
knew that Savannah had not done some of the things
that Lambeth had said she had, could not have done
them, and she knew she didn't believe it. But she had
decided to believe him anyway, and so she needed to

quarrel with Savannah, in order to make her decision even halfway appropriate, even if retroactively.

"You saw that I was out with Mr. Lambeth?"

Savannah stopped in the doorway to the hall. "Yes," she said. "I saw that."

"And you decided to say nothing? To just walk by?"

Savannah nodded. "I thought that might be the best way to handle an awkward situation."

"And why awkward? Is it because you believe that you are too good for a respectable man like Mr. Lambeth? And because of that you believe that everyone must join you in your disdain?"

Savannah flushed, but not with embarrassment. She started to feel herself getting angry, and spoke a few firm words to herself silently before she spoke. "Not at all, Elizabeth. I was going to say nothing because I believe that you are far too good for him."

That gave Elizabeth the opening she needed, and a torrent of hot words came out, in the kind of fierce whisper that women sometimes use. "You have always despised him, and have made that clear many times at table. You have always looked down on women who might not share your particular and peculiar tastes, and you have as much as said so. 'Pity the woman,' you once said, 'who takes up with that man.' 'Though,' you added, 'her one good fortune is likely to be that she is too dim to ever discover her misfortune.' Did you not say that?"

Savannah opened her mouth, and then closed it again. She had said that. She was too angry to reply,

and was also immediately conflicted about whether
or not she should have ever said anything like that.
She was sometimes far too tart for her own good.
"Good night, Elizabeth," she said, after a long pause.
"I will think about what you say. Good night." She
nodded curtly to her adversary, and made her way
down the hall.

As she walked down the hall, she went past the
boarded up room that was being remodeled after the
fire. She turned right to make her way to her room.
She walked in, shut the door softly but fiercely, and
sat on the edge of her bed. She was very upset with
Elizabeth, mostly for not seeing through Lambeth,
but secondly for seeing through her. Elizabeth's shaft
had gone home. Had she been thinking about Elizabeth when she had made that remark? Had she been
trying to make a point? Had she been *wanting* to score
Elizabeth off? And she was not even all that sure that
she wanted to apologize to Elizabeth even if she decided the charge was true, that she had been proud
and uncharitable.

Elizabeth sat on the edge of her bed thinking, and
sat perfectly still for about an hour. She had tried to
make it her practice, over the last several years, whenever anybody criticized her for anything, to take it seriously as a matter of principle—whether her first reaction was to take it seriously or not. In this instance,
she was trying to do that, but had to spend the first
ten minutes arguing herself into a frame of mind
that would even entertain that idea. Lambeth was so

obviously a bad man, and Elizabeth was so obviously
going counter to her own better judgment in agreeing
to see him, that the jab she had taken at Savannah's
comment from months ago was likely just arbitrary. If
Savannah gave it the time of day, if she sought Elizabeth's forgiveness for anything, it would just reinforce
all the wrong things, the things that Elizabeth should
not be paying attention to at all. It would actually hurt
Elizabeth if Savannah apologized.

But after about ten minutes, when her anger cooled
down, she found herself slowly rotating around to the
other view. It didn't matter whether an apology was
"good for" Elizabeth. What mattered is whether it was
owed. If owed, then it should be rendered to her. If
not, then not. That part was simple. But was it owed?
Savannah remembered making the comment that Elizabeth mentioned; she remembered it with great clarity.

Had anyone else been visiting that day, someone
Savannah might have been trying to impress? Had she
been feeling at all competitive with Elizabeth? She had
been aware on some level that Elizabeth was competing with her, but for what she did not know. Now it appeared to be for the good opinion of Lambeth. Perhaps
she was not competing with Elizabeth, but had simply
been annoyed at the fact that she was being competed
with. But had the jibe been in any way aimed at Elizabeth? After an hour of concentrated thinking and occasional praying, she decided it quite possibly had been.
It was too late to go and tap on Elizabeth's door, but
Savannah would go there first thing in the morning.

And so she did. As it turned out, it was the only thing she could have done that could have had any kind of impact on Elizabeth at all. Savannah rapped lightly on Elizabeth's door about a half an hour before breakfast, and when Elizabeth came to the door, still in her robe, Savannah spoke quietly and to the point.

"I thought a great deal about what you said last night, and I decided that my comment, the one you quoted to me, had been full of some kind of vainglory." Savannah noted briefly that she had chosen the same word that Pastor Thomas had used with her. "I would like to seek your forgiveness for making it. I have no doubt that there were other comments that I have made that you also noticed, and perhaps you placed them in the same category. If so, I would like to seek your forgiveness for those as well." The words came out fairly smoothly, having been rehearsed many times.

Savannah ceased, and waited quietly. Elizabeth stood there for a moment, and then simply nodded. Not curtly, but not warmly either. Savannah thanked her and turned away. Elizabeth shut the door and leaned against it. *That* bird was out of the cage, and she could not come down to breakfast until it was back in, which is why she was ten minutes late.

Alan Lambeth walked to the front of his bank that same morning, and greeted the sheriff, who was leaning on the wall next to the door. Lambeth was a bit early, and none of the tellers were there yet. Sheriff Barnes nodded to him courteously. "Alan," he said. Lambeth nodded back, unlocked the door, and gestured for the sheriff to go in first, which he did.

"How can I be of assistance?" he said.

"Well, it's like this," the sheriff said. "Normally I don't have any mysteries at all. Usually I have to deal with small crimes committed by even smaller minds, and it doesn't take a lot of brain work to get those gents sleeping over at my house. But right now, I have two big crimes, two big mysteries—that boarding house fire, and the murder of poor Todd. I am kind of beside myself, and am going around to all kinds of people asking all kinds of questions."

"And I am on your list?" Lambeth smiled, a little grimly. He could tell instantly that the sheriff was downplaying the importance of his questions—whether to surprise Lambeth with them, or fool him into thinking they were no big deal, he did not know.

"If so, fire away," he immediately said.

"After I talked to you last time," the sheriff said, "I went and visited Todd about it. He had an iron-clad alibi—he was down in Lewiston playing poker all night at Bill's place. Five men vouched for him, and three of the girls." The sheriff was watching Lambeth closely as he said this, and thought he saw him flinch. But he wasn't sure.

Lambeth smiled grimly and said, "Good thing I didn't swear to seeing him. I just thought the shadow looked like him." He shrugged. "And I might have been delirious. It was a long night, as I think I mentioned."

"One other thing," the sheriff said. "When I asked him about his hat—I had to ask him about it—he acknowledged it was his hat. I showed it to him. 'Yep,' he said. 'Bought that one in Baltimore. I left it in Lambeth's office by accident.'"

"No, sorry," Lambeth said. "I can't help you there, as much as I would love to. He would come here from time to time—we had a business deal in the works. But he never left his hat here. I can't imagine what game he was playing, telling you that he did."

The two men sat quietly for a moment.

Lambeth broke the silence. "I can ask the tellers. Maybe he left it on one of the chairs out in the foyer."

"Appreciate it." The sheriff got up to go. Lambeth stood up with him, hopped over to his crutch, and escorted him to the door.

They both went out into the main part of the bank, and Lambeth noted there were no customers. That being the case, he called the two tellers over. When they arrived, Lambeth cleared his throat. One of the tellers was Taylor, who lived at the boarding house, and who had been so informative and helpful to Savannah in how she came to view Alan Lambeth.

"The sheriff here wants to know if Todd Martin—you remember? The gent that was shot?—Did he ever leave his hat here? Maybe on one of the chairs by the window?"

Both tellers shook their heads *no*, but Taylor's eyebrows went up a little, at least on the inside of his forehead. Martin had never sat out in the waiting area, he always walked straight in to see Lambeth. If Lambeth was busy with someone, Martin would just leave and come back later. And that hat—it had been an object of conversation more than once—was quite distinctive. And Taylor remembered Lambeth walking out of the bank with it recently. He thought it was curious at the time, and now thought it was even more curious that Lambeth was pretending that it might have been left out here. Taylor made a mental note to drop by and see the sheriff later, which he did that evening. The sheriff took notes and was most appreciative.

Elizabeth was getting ready to see Alan Lambeth again. He had called, quite courteously, in just the same way he had stopped in on her at David's the first time. "There is nowhere in town to take a lady," he said apologetically. "I thought we could go to the same restaurant and just order something different off the menu. Maybe sit at a different table."

She laughed out loud. "That will be quite pleasant," she said.

Inside she didn't know what to do. There were at least three of her having an argument with the other two. Savannah's apology that morning put the lie to what Lambeth had told her last night about Savannah. Her years with Savannah had already told her the same thing, but the apology had sealed it. There is no way the Savannah that Elizabeth knew would have been capable of something like what Alan Lambeth said. The second version of Elizabeth didn't care if it was all a lie. She wanted to believe the lie, knowing it to be a lie, and she had no other reason for the malicious desire than that Savannah's teeth were so straight, and that her figure was not. The third Elizabeth simply wanted Lambeth to court her, regardless of his intentions or motives. She had wanted this innocently enough a few years earlier, had never let go of it, and now it did not appear it was going to let go of her.

After they were at dinner, Lambeth artfully—and he was artful—brought the subject around to Savannah again. "My sincere regrets in doing this," he said, "but could I ask you to pass a message on to that woman?" Elizabeth sat quietly, her face showing no sign of the tumult going on below. After a moment, which Lambeth quite misunderstood, she nodded her head and said, "Certainly. I trust you have a good reason for asking me to do something like this?"

"I do," he said.

He did misunderstand what was going on within her. He thought he was in danger of wounding her vanity by giving too much importance to her one-time rival. But the issue was with her charity or sense of fair play, or at least what was left of it. She kept going back and forth in her soul, rocking between her desire to be with Lambeth, a goal she had had for several years now, and her faintly receding awareness that he was plainly lying to her about Savannah. She was managing this by resolutely refusing to think about both issues at the same time.

She turned away from what she knew to be true the third time. "What is the message?" She smiled faintly as she asked.

He became a little more solemn. "We both knew the unfortunate Mr. Martin, as I believe you know. We had some independent business with him. As my relations with Sav . . . her . . . are now . . . frosty . . . I need someone I can trust to give her a message about him. I don't want to deal with her directly at all any more."

"And the message?"

"The message doesn't mean anything to me, but the last time I saw Todd, he asked me to let Savannah know 'that Milwaukee was an open question.' I haven't an earthly notion what that might mean, but I told him I would tell her—it was right before that last trip of his, and I am afraid I forgot to do it. But now that he has passed, and I remembered it just yesterday, I feel obligated."

"I think your thoughtfulness does you justice. Especially after how she has treated you." That is what she managed to say. Inside she was fuming. That makes no sense at all. Why would Todd Martin ask Alan to give Savannah a message?

"Well," he said, "I did give my word."

Elizabeth passed the message on to Savannah that same night. Savannah was in the sitting room alone when Elizabeth got back, and so she simply stopped by Savannah's chair, and told her. Savannah nodded her head briefly, and said, "Thank you." She registered no emotion at all, although Elizabeth, her curiosity piqued about her message, was watching her closely.

But the reason Savannah showed no emotion is that earlier that day she had gotten a letter from Todd Martin. It had of course startled her when she opened

it and glanced at the signature—there had been no return address on the envelope—and so she had then
read the letter through several times carefully. She had
been pondering it ever since.

Todd Martin was a single and unattached man, and
so he—as he briefly explained in the letter—had kept a
small box of valuables at the company headquarters in
Chicago. It would have been more convenient if he had
kept it at his house, but his grandparents had once lost
many of their valuable records in a fire, and so he had
kind of a superstition about living in the same place
where such things were located. The box contained
his will, a few other oddments, and several letters to
be posted upon his death. On his last trip east, he had
written this letter, and sent it sealed to a friend there
at headquarters, and asked him to throw it in his box.

The letter to Savannah was short, about three pag-
es. In it he explained his system, meaning the box back
at headquarters, he explained that he was at peace with
God, inexplicably, and third, that if she got this letter it
would be because he was dead, and that Lambeth had
done him in. "If I die," he wrote, "and there is anything
whatever mysterious about the circumstances of my
death, you can lay even money on the fact that Lambeth was behind it." And of course, Savannah already
knew this, but it was still eerie for her to be reading
this letter from a murdered man, calmly discussing his
future murder.

The point of the letter, Martin went on, was to assure her that if he died in mysterious circumstances,

her secret was absolutely secure, and that there would be absolutely no one in Paradise who knew about it, least of all Lambeth. "I know him," Martin wrote, "and he will no doubt try to bluff something, or some way through, but don't you believe it."

And so when Savannah heard Elizabeth calmly delivering a cryptic message, she calmly listened, and nodded. She believed not a word.

DINNER IN
PARADISE

Little strokes fell great oaks.
BEN FRANKLIN

The mayor had been attending all the booster events throughout the region, and had done so with an almost religious devotion. He was a medieval pilgrim, wending his way to *all* the shrines. He loved all such events, even when the people involved were boosting causes or municipalities that were not dear to his heart. What was dear to his heart was the idea of boosterism, the spirit of it. The friend of one saintly finger bone needed to be, in some measure, a friend to all of them.

Wherever he went, he gathered ideas and inspiration. He would look around and see men and women who were proficient in their craft and who knew how to bring people on board. He had been doing this for many months, steeling and preparing himself for the time when he would prevail on his own Chamber of Commerce to host a magnificent event right there in Paradise. He waited until he felt a certain inevitability to it, and then put it on the calendar.

He successfully sold the idea to the Chamber, and then to the city council, who agreed to underwrite the cost of the banquet. He timed it so that the governor could make it. He coordinated with the university president, who was interested in the mayor's help on a funding appeal to the state board of education. He got the backing of the big merchants in town, who helped to underwrite the advertising for the whole affair. No one need worry about losing any money on it, at least not on the first one. Everyone knew that this was a big roll of the dice, and if the mayor won, then they all won. If it was a dud, then they would all know it was not yet their time. The mayor's hope was that it would put all the other regional banquets and balls into the shade. This should become the annual event that everyone would have to make a point never to miss. As social events go, the mayor wanted Paradise to be second only to Spokane, and they couldn't be expected to compete with Spokane anyhow.

Anyone in Paradise who had any social standing at all received an engraved invitation. And all the people that the mayor would take anywhere else in order to show off Paradise were included, and were included in the first instance. In fact, the mayor had his wife sound Savannah out about her willingness to serve as the official hostess of the affair. He thought—wisely—that his wife would take it amiss if he asked her directly and, as a prudent man, he lined up all the arrangements for the head table in quite a reasonable way.

The governor and his wife would be seated in the center, of course; Savannah would be seated to the left of the governor's wife, and he, the mayor, with his wife would be on the governor's right. Down the table were other worthies—the president of the chamber with spouse, the university president with spouse, and so on. Taking one thing with another, the line-up of the head table, with the notable exception of Savannah, was a well-groomed collection of dignified eyesores. Savannah kind of stood out, and a number of people had already decided instinctively where they would be looking during the course of the speeches and toasts. And there, to Savannah's left, was an empty chair that would belong to the winner of the first raffle event of the evening, the one that would happen right after everyone was first seated.

His wife had thought of that, and the mayor thought it was a fantastic idea. Raffle off a distinguished spot at the head table, three down from the governor, and right next to the prettiest woman in the room. He hoped vaguely that a man would win it, and that the man's wife would not be too upset with him.

He began to have misgivings about the whole thing. Perhaps he hadn't thought this all the way through.

But his misgivings didn't show. "Before you get settled," the mayor boomed in his stentorian way, "we will have a surprise raffle. Look under your coffee cup, and you will find your raffle ticket there. I will read out the number, twice, and the lucky winner will make his or her way down to the head table here, and dine with us!" And slowly, deliberately, he did just as he had said. He read out the number.

Mrs. Fuller's heart sank momentarily when she realized that her number was the winning ticket. She could visit with Savannah anytime. But then inspiration suddenly struck. "Let me see your ticket," she said to Pastor Thomas, who was sitting right next to her. She took it readily, gazed at it eagerly, and then returned her own ticket to Thomas, acting disappointed with the ticket she kept. She would seek forgiveness later, at some more appropriate time.

Their two tickets were only different by one digit, and so it was easy, when the mayor read out the number again for her to nudge Thomas and say, "What is your number?" Thomas looked at it, started furiously, looked at it again, and then up at Savannah. He stood up and started to make his way to the head table. He noticed that she had flushed crimson as soon as she saw him stand. Whether from anger or some other emotional forces, he did not know. This should be interesting.

He wound his way through the tables, applauded by half of the crowd out of simple courtesy, and by the other half, a bit more enthusiastic, this second half made up of members of that contingent which thought Thomas and Savannah should be a couple. That number had been growing recently, particularly among the Presbyterians. Everybody appeared to see it except for the principals.

Thomas walked around the head table on the right side, stepped up on the dais, walked down to the mayor and handed him his ticket. The mayor took it with mock seriousness, pretended to read it, and then announced to everyone that there had been no signs of cheating. The crowd laughed uproariously. This was partly because everyone had arrived in a mood for a good time, partly because Thomas was a clergyman, and partly because they thought the mayor was getting in a sly dig at the expense of Thomas and Savannah.

As Thomas sat down next to her, Mrs. Fuller gazed at them both in stark amazement. You foolish girl, she thought. Whatever it is, you cannot argue with anything like *that*. She wondered briefly if she had gone astray theologically. Presbyterians believed in predestination, and it seemed suspect to her that she was kind of helping predestination along. She would have to ask Pastor Thomas about the theology of it sometime.

Pastor Thomas bowed slightly to Savannah, who was already seated, and said, "Well, this is delightful." He was all manners, genuinely warm. His earlier bout with despair had only lasted for three days, but it was still right there, just under the surface. His confidence was sincere enough to be convincing to her.

While he was coming up to the head table, she had decided, firmly and with all the resolve she had, that she would be courteous, friendly, and tart. If he thought he could just come walking up and spend the evening joking around with her like they were old chums, up here in front of just about everybody, then he was in for a surprise. She felt as though she were on the verge of a fencing match, and she had been flexing her rapier.

"I am glad you find it delightful," she said. "Did you cheat to win the prize? I really don't think a clergyman ought to cheat at anything, even something as trivial as this." At this she flashed a bright smile, the kind that said it would be impermissible to take offense at anything that was said.

"Oh, no, I wouldn't cheat at something trivial, and I wouldn't cheat at something that meant a great deal to me. And this happy event is certainly one of those." Parry, thrust.

She knew he was pursuing her, and had known that for some time. But in these first few exchanges, they had both crossed an important boundary line. She knew that he was pursuing her, but she now knew that *he* knew that she knew that he was. It was as though it was the most obvious thing in the world, sitting there on the white tablecloth in between their two plates. They both saw it, and they each saw that the other saw it. The unspoken words in everything they were saying were unspoken only to anyone who happened to walk behind them. Such an outsider would have understood nothing. But the two of them were both coming to understand everything.

"Judging from your sermon two weeks ago, you don't believe in chance. You did a wonderful job of explaining how 'time and chance happen to them all' does nothing to touch the sovereignty of God. I wonder then at your participation in a raffle."

"Oh, I would never buy a raffle ticket. But this was just thrust upon me."

"Do Presbyterians approve of participating in games of chance? Are you setting a good example for the flock? Participating in a raffle?" She returned to press the point.

He grinned. "There was no chance involved. I have a system. It isn't gambling if you have a sure-fire system."

"I see. I already asked if you were cheating. What possible system could you have for a raffle if you weren't cheating?"

"It is called," he said, "trusting God. Delighting in the Lord."

That stopped her cold, and so, stalling for time, she asked, "And how is this system supposed to work?"

"If you delight yourself in the Lord," he said evenly, looking straight into her eyes, "He will give you the desires of your heart. Psalm 37:4."

They looked straight at each other for a moment, and Savannah broke her gaze first. "That doesn't always work for both parties," she said. She said this in such a way as to make him wonder if they were not desiring the same thing, or if she was not interested in him, or if she did desire what he did, and God was not interested in giving her anything, much less the desires of her heart.

For a moment, Thomas wavered. There was something there that made him want to answer like a pastor instead of like a suitor. But he decided it was a distraction, and pressed on. Pastoral concerns could wait.

She felt what was happening before she knew what it was. She was being tart, in both manner and word, and the words alone should have been discouraging to him. But she also knew, somewhere deep in her soul, that she was also flirting. She was standing over the pancakes again, with Mrs. Fuller looking balefully across the kitchen at her. That earlier time she had wanted him to know how good a cook she was, and now—though she was saying things that ought to have put him off—she actually wanted him to ignore the content of what she was saying and, as a disinterested critic, admire the wit in it. She wanted him to approve of her disapproval of him. She wanted him to notice how quick she was, and she knew that she was planting explosives underneath her stated strategy. She wanted him to ignore everything she was doing, and focus instead on how well she was doing it. But she wasn't doing it well at all and . . . *bother*.

But as she wanted him to admire how quick she was, he was gratifying her wish, and he was noticing exactly that.

Wanting to hear a good deal more from her, he started to speak again, but was interrupted by the mayor.

"And because we already have a clergyman up here on the dais, I am wondering if we might prevail upon Pastor Goforth to ask the blessing for us. That is, if he can tear himself away from the lovely Miss Westmoreland." The mayor laughed at himself, mightily pleased. He was the kind of man who thought that he never gave offense because people liked him enough to forgive him for a great deal. The crowd laughed again, some of them nervously this time.

Pastor Thomas approached the lectern slowly, carefully. The mayor did not know how inappropriate he was being, and Thomas was thinking quickly, his mind racing. He needed to say something that would derail the mayor's apparent theme for the evening, and he needed to do it in a way that didn't reinforce the theme of his joking, and also in a way that did not make Savannah uncomfortable in other ways.

He thought of what to say just as he got to the podium. "Before we say grace, let me say just a quick word about the mayor's understandable mistake. As some of you may know, at the Presbyterian church we have a building campaign coming up, and I was just talking to Miss Westmoreland about possibly donating to it. I haven't been long here in Paradise, but I had already heard how much the teachers are paid by this district."

His diversion was a complete success. The pay of teachers in the district was notoriously low, almost scandalous, and to the mayor's credit, he had been one of the most vocal men in the community in agitating for a change. But it was a point on which he was sensitive, especially at a banquet designed to showcase to outsiders all things Paradise. He colored slightly, and his comments for the rest of the evening ran in a much more edifying direction.

After Pastor Thomas was done with his prayer, he returned to his seat and sat down quietly, unsure of his reception. Savannah leaned toward him slightly and said, "If I may declare a momentary truce—only momentary, mind you—I would like to say thank you. That was nicely done."

"I am glad you noticed it, and you are most welcome." Pastor Thomas said. "My only qualm is that I may have come perilously close to violating the ninth commandment."

"Oh, everyone knows that you weren't asking me for money."

"Yes, but I did it so that they would stop thinking something else. And what I wanted them to stop thinking about was what I actually was doing. That was not so much a change of subject, or a joke, but a successful misdirection. One need not tell a lie in order to deceive. Suppose I were to tell someone that this banquet was a great success, in part because the mayor showed up sober. There would not be a word of untruth in it, but the impression created would be entirely false. That is the sort of thing that worries me in this instance. I successfully got the assembled here to stop thinking about how I am paying you attention of a particular kind. And yet, truth be told, if you were to examine my motives closely . . ."

Her eyes got a little wider, and they flashed for a moment. "And I," she said, "think that you are violating a solemn truce. One that I declared in good faith."

"Yes, quite. It was a truce, but I had thought your words were 'momentary truce.'"

Pastor Thomas was greatly encouraged at how the conversation had been going. Not only had Savannah come to understand the two levels of what she was doing, but so had Thomas. He knew that there was an important place in her life where his attentions were not unwelcome. He knew also that something was in the way, but he believed that it could be dealt with and removed. At least he believed that in the moment. Doubts and despair were reserved for two in the morning. But whatever that was, whatever it took, he intended to be a participant.

"Ah, yes," he said. "So you did. But I have a lot of things on my mind. Actually that is not true. I only have one thing on my mind."

"Pastor Thomas!" she said. "We both understand each other, I believe, but I really must insist that we continue to speak . . . to speak in code."

"Wonderful," he said. "A secret language. Just the two of us?"

Savannah icily turned her attentions to her salad, which had just arrived. She gestured toward his salad, which had immediately followed. "I believe that your attentions are more likely to be accommodated there. I suggest you devote yourself to it, and you will be amply rewarded. I wouldn't want you to get discouraged."

"I have no intention of getting, as you so quaintly put it, discouraged. What could possibly be discouraging? I came to a wonderful dinner without a companion, the only glum spot in the whole affair, and the first thing that happened upon my arrival is that I won a raffle—one I didn't even enter, so as to satisfy the sternest of critics among my parishioners—and the prize for this unsought for raffle is that I was brought up here to the head table, just like in the parable, and was given a seat that is located right next to . . . this wonderful salad."

His timing was impeccable. Just as he said right next to, she sat up straight, starting to get truly indignant, but collapsed at the word *salad*.

They both ate silently for a few moments, and then Pastor Thomas spoke again. "Let me propose the truce this time. Suppose we spend the rest of the evening in pleasant banter, on any subject whatever, and we both agree to have no hidden meanings in what we say, at least not on purpose. We both have a very pleasant evening."

"Go on," she said.

"In exchange," he said, "we agree that we will have a serious talk, sometime soon, where we may both speak freely to each other. When that time comes—and I will see that it comes in the next week or so—there will be no evasions or pretenses. Each of us will have permission of the other to say whatever we believe must be said."

A feeling of dread closed in on her, but she knew there was no way out. She nodded.

The rest of the evening, despite the dread, was one she enjoyed very much indeed.

THE TRAIN
THAT LEFT

And I'm already gone . . .
THE EAGLES

Savannah was sitting in Mrs. Fuller's bedroom later that night, fuming. "I think he must have arranged all of that with the mayor. What are the odds of him winning that seat in an honest raffle?"

"Now, dearie," said Mrs. Fuller.

"And when he came up and sat down up there, he was just *full* of double meanings. Filled and overflowing. Everything he said was about the two of us."

179

"Everything?"

"Well, it was until he quit talking about it. But he only quit on the condition that I agree to talk with him about . . . about us. He said it would be within the next week or so."

Mrs. Fuller nodded. "That was gentlemanly of him. That gives you time to think about how best to respond . . ."

"Gentlemanly!?" she exploded. "I have little doubt that when I am walking to school tomorrow morning, he is going to jump out of the bushes on the way and offer to chat. I am not going to have time to think through anything."

"I am sure that . . ."

Savannah interrupted. "I think he had to have arranged it with the mayor."

Mrs. Fuller decided that the time for confession had come. "No, Savannah. He didn't arrange anything. My ticket was the winning ticket. I asked to see his, and returned mine to him instead. He had no idea, and neither did the mayor."

Savannah tried hard to glare at her friend, but then looked down, half smiling. "I should have known he was not the cheater. Not when *you* were in the room."

"Dearie, it is the sort of thing I might ordinarily feel bad about. But as soon as I saw the two of you sitting up there, looking like the king and queen in a fairy tale, I knew that I had done the right thing."

"But this is all beside the point. What will I say to him?"

TH E   TR A I N   T H AT   LE F T

"I don't know what precisely, but I think it should be something that results in him sitting by you like that a lot more."

"You are a dear friend, but really, dear friends ought to be a lot more helpful."

***

Lambeth decided that he was going to have to guess. He thought he knew the ways of the world well enough, and he sat down with a pad of paper at his kitchen table, and spent an evening working through what he thought were the possibilities. Martin had seen her, and so it had to have been in a place where Martin could have been. That meant it was either in a business setting, or at a tavern, or perhaps a combination. He knew from other visits with Martin that he would take clients and prospects out to dinners, or drinks, and what was more likely than that he had met Savannah in some place like that—mistress to one of the businessmen he was pursuing. He had to have known her well enough to know that she was in an unsavory position.

He then spent a great deal of time crafting a sentence that would greatly unsettle Savannah if true, and which would not display a total lack of knowledge on his part if he had guessed wrong.

The following day he walked up to the school again, an hour or so after school let out, just as he had done the first time. Again he walked down the long hall to Savannah's room. His cast had only been off for a few days, and so his gait was not as confident as the first time he came. This time she did not see or hear him coming.

He tapped on the door lightly as he came in. Savannah was sitting at her desk, grading papers. She sat back in her chair, and looked expectantly at him.

"I thought it would be only right to tell you that I have discovered the name of your gentleman friend," he said.

Savannah did the best thing she could have done under the circumstances. She laughed out loud, and without speaking, turned back to her papers.

***

Pastor Thomas walked slowly up to the front of the bank, thought briefly again about what he intended to do, drew in two short breaths and exhaled one short prayer, turned the knob, and went in.

He was greeted cheerfully by the tellers, who liked Pastor Thomas very much.

"Is Mr. Lambeth free?" Thomas asked.

"Let me check," one of them, the youngest, said. "I think so." With that, he bounded over to the glassed-in office that served for Lambeth's quarters, peered through the glass, tapped lightly on it, and stuck his head through the door. He briefly exchanged words with somebody in there, indicating that it was probably Lambeth, and then came back out.

"Yes, he is. He will see you in just a few minutes."

Pastor Thomas nodded briefly, and took a seat. He thumbed absently through a magazine that had been there for several years, and then stood up when Alan Lambeth came out.

He greeted Thomas courteously enough, but not heartily. After the initial greetings, his eyebrows went up inquisitively. Pastor Thomas nodded toward his office, as much as to say that he would like to speak privately. Lambeth shrugged, and walked back to his office, with Thomas following.

When they were settled, Lambeth spread out his hands with a mock courtesy. "How," he asked, "may I help you?"

"I came," Thomas said, "to follow up on the conversation we had at the church after the incident at the picnic. I gathered from your response at that time you had no intention of apologizing to Miss Westmoreland, but I thought I would be remiss in my duties if I did not come back after a suitable period of time to ask you again."

Lambeth snorted. "I do like one thing about you, Pastor Galahad. You do have unvarnished gall. No, of course I do not intend to apologize for anything."

Pastor Thomas continued smoothly. "I have been meaning to drop in on you for some weeks now, but things have been hectic. The reason I came in today is that I just happened to see you walking away from the school. I am glad to see your cast off, at any rate. On the supposition that you may have been there to see Miss Westmoreland, it occurred to me that I ought to come by and ask you if that was the case. If it was,

I was going to ask you to discontinue any further attempts to talk with her."

Lambeth grinned icily. "Like I said, unvarnished gall. I have said everything I intend to say to her, and devil take her. But I am almost persuaded to go speak to her one more time, and attribute the need for it to our little visit here."

"Well," said Thomas as he stood, "At least I think we have reached our understanding."

***

Savannah walked down the long hallway that led to Elizabeth's room, and softly tapped on the door. After a moment, the door opened a crack and Elizabeth peered out.

"May I visit with you for a moment?" Savannah asked. "I would like to come in, if I might."

Elizabeth stood silently, and then, without expression, opened the door wide. "Come in," she said.

The room was spacious, much like Savannah's, and Elizabeth had a small sitting area with two chairs and a small table between them. Elizabeth gestured, not ungraciously, to the nearest chair. Savannah hesitated and then sat down. Elizabeth sat down across from her, and pursed her lips slightly, as much as to say, "Well?"

Savannah cleared her throat and began. "Elizabeth, I did not come to try actively to persuade you of anything, or to get you to agree to anything. I simply felt bound in my conscience to *tell* you something, and to leave it there with you to do as you will."

"That sounds fair enough," Elizabeth said.

"I am not in a position to prove anything that I am about to say, and so I cannot produce any evidence that could reasonably satisfy you. All I can do is ask you to take these things into account as a possibility."

"Go on," Elizabeth said. Her face was neither soft nor hard. It just was.

"The only other thing before I say what I came to say is this. Please reflect on the fact that I could not possibly receive any benefit from talking to you about this, one way or the other. Whatever it is I am doing, it achieves nothing for me personally."

"I will just have to take your word for that, I suppose," Elizabeth said.

The two women sat quietly for a moment.

"When I turned down Mr. Lambeth's advances last year, it was simply because I was nervous about his character from things I had heard—you heard them too, around the table. But it was nothing more than not wanting to be courted by someone who might be such a man. However, in subsequent events—at the picnic, and in other ways that I will not go into—not being able to prove them—I have since come to the conclusion that Mr. Lambeth is a very bad man. I believe that he is simply using you to get back at me for some reason, and I believe that you are very likely in danger."

Elizabeth's eyebrows shot up. "*Danger*? You think that Alan killed that Martin fellow?"

Savannah colored slightly. That was in fact the conclusion she wanted Elizabeth to draw without being called upon to prove anything. "I didn't say that," she said. "But I do believe you are in danger."

***

Alan Lambeth had misjudged his woman. He had thought, quite rightly, that Elizabeth was open to scoring Savannah off, and was sorely tempted by the opportunity to do so, but he had miscalculated how robust her conscience was. She was susceptible to everything that Lambeth was going to use on her, but she was not really all that susceptible at the rate he was going. She was having to acclimatize to a great deal of corruption all at once, and she was frankly making heavy weather of it.

She had been thinking all day about Savannah's warning. The only possible selfish motive she could conceive for it was the possibility of sour grapes. But Savannah had been the one who had rejected Lambeth, not the other way around. And Elizabeth knew she was not interpreting Lambeth's behavior as possible sour grapes, though there was objective reason for thinking that. And Savannah's sincere apology a few nights before—if anything had ever been sincere, *that* was—had been very difficult for Elizabeth to fit into any story with Savannah as the villain.

Elizabeth had struggled with all of this for the better part of a day. She had another date with Lam— with Alan that night, and she found herself worrying about it. As she was walking home, she met Mrs. Fuller walking away from the boardinghouse. She had forgotten baking soda on her previous trip to the store, and it was required for dinner. The grocer's was just a block away, and they didn't close until five.

The two women passed each other with a pleasant greeting—Elizabeth liked Mrs. Fuller—and a few steps past her, she stopped.

"Mrs. Fuller," she said.

Mrs. Fuller stopped and turned around. "Yes?"

"May I ask you a personal question?"

"Certainly, dear."

"I understand from several people that you were there at the picnic when Savannah threw the bowl at Mr. Lambeth?"

"So I was," the older woman replied.

"What was the cause of that?"

Mrs. Fuller stood motionless for a moment, and then leaned forward and whispered in Elizabeth's ear.

***

"May I speak with you for a moment, miss?" The voice belonged to Sheriff Barnes, and the young woman was Elizabeth, standing behind the counter at David's. She nodded, and so the sheriff continued.

"Is there a place where we can speak privately?"

Elizabeth shook her head. "No, but this is quite all right. Sally has gone to lunch, and this time of day is always quiet. No one else is here."

The sheriff had taken off his hat when he came in, and he was rubbing the bald spot on the back of his head somewhat nervously. "May I request permission to speak somewhat personally? More than I usually would in the course of my duties?"

"Certainly. I am sure you would not take any liberties . . ."

The sheriff interrupted her. "No, no, certainly not . . . Well, it is like this, miss. This is a small town, and people talk, they do. I happen to know that Mr. Lambeth has been paying you some attention, and that kind of thing is really not my business, really it is not. But in this instance, I just wanted to tell you to be careful. Just be careful. I don't want to say much more than that, as it wouldn't be proper. But it never hurts to be careful."

Elizabeth fixed him with her coldest stare. "Indeed it does not hurt to be careful. I want always to be careful. Careful of what?"

The sheriff had decided before he had come in what he would do if Elizabeth showed herself resistant to what he was saying. It was just a word to the wise. He wasn't going to try to convince her of anything. Not if she didn't want to hear it. No, not at all.

"Just be careful of Mr. Lambeth. There is more to him than you might think." And with that the sheriff put his hat back on, and walked to the door while trying to look as though he was not walking mysteriously. He almost succeeded.

***

At dinner, Lambeth was open and gracious, or at least seemed to be so. Despite having acted in a noncommittal way with both of them, Elizabeth had been badly rattled by Savannah's visit, and then by Sheriff Barnes' warning. She knew what she wanted, and she had wanted it for several years now. But as she reflected—as much as she permitted herself to reflect, which was not very much—she was starting to wonder why she had wanted it.

At the back of her mind, asking for admittance, was the idea that she wanted Lambeth, not because she wanted Lambeth, but because she needed to best Savannah at *something*. And even that didn't make sense because if she took up with Lambeth after Savannah had brushed him off, in what way was that winning? How was it not coming in second place, even on the supposition that Lambeth was a catch?

Lambeth was a place holder for her rivalry with Savannah, and she simultaneously knew this, and refused to know it. And then Savannah's visit, her self-evident care and love for her—a love she did not think she returned at all—and her inability to figure out any possible selfish motive Savannah might have possessed—had put Elizabeth in a state of suspended consternation. And that was how she had been when the sheriff had arrived to talk to her.

All in all, Elizabeth was by now extremely wary of Lambeth. She would have to be a fool not to be wary, and she was no fool. And yet, though she was no fool, she had been a prisoner of the sidelong glance her entire life. It was the deepest point of common contact between her and Lambeth. Before Savannah it had been that woman at college, and before that, her older sister.

And the sidelong glance is not something that can be just switched off.

Lambeth pulled her chair back for her magnanimously, and she smiled at him over her shoulder. She didn't know why she was smiling.

After dinner, he walked Elizabeth back toward the boardinghouse. As they came to an intersection, about three blocks from home, he took her hand and squeezed it a little bit harder than gentle.

"My home is just up the road here," he said, nodding to the left. "We could go up there for a little while. It is fairly secluded."

She pretended to not know what he meant, and she shook her head as though she had misunderstood him. "Straight ahead is the best way home," she said lamely.

With that, he bent over and kissed her, harder than he needed to, and hard enough to make it impossible for her to misunderstand. He pulled back and nodded up the road again.

She knew that she couldn't pretend anymore, and she also knew, quite suddenly, that she couldn't do it.

"Not yet," she said, after a moment. "I really have to get back tonight. Tomorrow?" she said. She looked up at him, she hoped longingly, with her right hand on his chest.

He nodded. "Tomorrow would work wonderfully."

They turned and started walking back toward the boardinghouse, now holding hands. She hoped that he couldn't feel her pulse pounding in her wrist. Or if he did, maybe he would attribute it to passion.

As they approached the house, he brought something else up, quite nonchalantly. "Would you mind passing one more thing on to your housemate? I promise to be done after that."

"Well, after tomorrow night, I should be able to promise you *anything*. And that means tonight I should be able to pass on a simple message. You must have some good reason." She looked up at him again.

"I remembered one other thing that Martin had said," Lambeth said. "It had something to do with the train station. Something about meeting her there once. It is meaningless to me, of course, and I feel funny passing pointless messages from a dead man to an enemy. But there it is."

Elizabeth looked up at him again, and she knew, instantly, while not sure how she knew, that Lambeth was taunting Savannah. He was not passing on any message. And she also suddenly knew that he had been the one who had shot Martin. And now he was threatening Savannah, and Savannah knew it, and Savannah had *still* tried to warn her.

They came to the front walk running up to the boarding house. Elizabeth leaned forward and kissed him warmly. "That should tide you over. I want you to spend at least a quarter of your time at work tomorrow thinking about tomorrow night."

He smiled in the dusk, a little too eagerly she thought. She shivered when she saw his teeth glint momentarily in the moonlight. "Oh, it will be more than *half* my time at work," he said.

"Don't forget the message," he said. "Train station."

"Yes," she said. "Yes. I will tell her."

With that lie, she turned and ran up the stairs to the front door, and then up the stairs again to her room. Without losing a second, she pulled her suitcase out of her closet and began throwing her essential things into it. Whatever would fit in the case would go, and whatever would not fit would remain. She knew that there was a train at nine o clock, and she would catch it. It did not matter where it was going. She would figure out where she would stop once she was out of this town.

TURMOIL IN TOWN

It ain't what you don't know that gets you into trouble.
It's what you know for sure that just ain't so.

MARK TWAIN

Forrest Sampson was walking downtown like he
had just paid off the mortgage for all the build-
ings in the entire downtown. Exuberance does not begin to describe what was going on inside him. After
many months of agonizing in his soul over his love
for Miss Eleanor Simpson, and having spent three
sleepless nights in a row, he had in final desperation
decided that he was going to have to declare himself.
He was going to lose his job otherwise—he worked at
the feed store, and several times the previous week he

had botched some routine and ordinary orders, and they weren't small orders either, and he had done so because—as he acknowledged frankly to himself—he had been daydreaming about his love for Eleanor. In fairness it should be noted that he acknowledged this to himself only because it was yet another way of continuing to think about her.

In the build up to today's marvelous turn of events, he had had no doubt in his mind that it was not going to be marvelous at all. He was not worthy of Miss Simpson, a plain fact which the entire world must know and acknowledge. And if the tawdry and cynical world knew this, how could Eleanor, in all her radiant wisdom, *not* know it? But despite this knowledge, he could not talk himself into a reasonable resignation. He was hopeless and he knew it. And the thought had occurred to him, just that morning, that hopeless despair after having been rejected *might* be something he could handle better than the hopeless despair of unspoken, and therefore necessarily unrequited, love. "I know I can't do *this* anymore," he had said to himself. "Maybe I can handle the despair after she crushes me. Maybe certain despair is easier than uncertain despair."

And so this is what he had just done an hour before. He had felt as though he were going up before an implacable and terrible feminine tribunal. In his imagination, he was going to walk up to a table, with her standing behind it, a stern and beautiful expression on her face. He was going to spread all his innards out on the table before her, and he was then going to give her a huge wooden mallet, and she would do as she pleased. Given the high insult his declaration of love would naturally be to someone as noble as she was, he was confident that she would wield that heavy mallet with a will. And yet he loved her still. He sincerely believed she was going to destroy him without ceasing to be the most wonderful woman in the world . . . filled with kindness and tenderly overflowing with it.

It was his day off, and so he had walked around to the laundry where she worked, across the street from the bank, and walked in. There she was, standing behind the counter, her blue company apron on, hair up in a bun with a pencil stuck in it, and with suds on her hands. Forrest had never seen anything so lovely in his life, and he almost lost his nerve. Several of Eleanor's co-workers were standing in the back, next to the tubs, and they both tittered and whispered something to each other. She came up to the counter, willing to talk with *him*, and Forrest asked to speak with her out in the alley, and he did this while managing to keep too much of a quaver out of his voice.

When they were finally out back—getting there seemed like an eternity to him—he found himself looking at the dirt under his feet, and wishing he were down there with his feet. "Yes?" she said, all friendliness. Haltingly, inadequately, fearfully, he got it out. Well, he got most of it out. He had (scores of times) rehearsed what he would ever say if ever he got the nerve to say it, and he is to be commended that he only forgot about a third of it. But she was bright as well as pretty, and she nevertheless got the gist. He loved her. That was just the way it was, darn it.

He was still looking down at his boots, as though he had been courting *them*, and so he had been beyond astonished when Miss Eleanor Simpson had simply burst into tears, thrown her arms around his neck, and accepted him. Just like that.

It took him a few moments to recover himself. He was sure that he had lost his mind in all the stress, and that his hallucinations had decided to torment him with false and vivid hopes. When it finally came crashing in upon him that she was in fact holding him tightly around the neck, that she was weeping with joy, and that she had kissed him two or three times, he too entered into joy.

No, he didn't have a ring. He had money for a ring though, and they could go look for one as soon as may be. He had thought actually buying a ring would have been presumptuous. He was *ready* to buy a ring and that would prevent him being guilty of the high presumption of actually doing so. He thought through all of this very carefully, multiple times. He had almost delivered his declaration three times before, but each time had faltered and shuddered to a stop.

"You are a very silly man," she said, patting his shoulder. "I am sure I have loved you for as long as you have loved me, and once I knew how you felt, which has been the last six months or so, I tried everything I could think of—within the boundaries of propriety—to let you know that I felt the same way. But you wouldn't let me help you . . . you wouldn't even look me in the eye . . ."

"I couldn't," Forrest said. "I thought about it a few times, but I was afraid I would have a heart attack or something really bad. I was terrible afraid of taking liberties."

Eleanor laughed, and her laugh was merry, full of relief. "That last time you almost proposed, do you remember?"

Forrest stared at her, mystified. "I remember everything about it. I was in agony. But how did you know about it?" He was amazed at her insight and wisdom, and told her so.

She laughed again. "There was nothing insightful about it at all. Remember, it was the night after the big banquet at the Odd Fellows. We were working late here because they needed all those rented tablecloths the next night at St. Mary's. The girls teased me about it something fearful." A moment later she added, "It was the same night as that fire, I remember."

"Teased you? But why?"

"Why? Because you were pacing up and down the street, north and south, north and south, and something always kept you from just coming *in*. I almost ran out several times to see if kissing you would help you understand."

Forrest laughed awkwardly. The world was apparently running on certain principles and possibilities that he had not taken into account at all. *Nothing* was the way he had thought it was.

And so now it was about an hour later, an hour after
he had had all his misconceptions destroyed—*he* was not
destroyed, his misconceptions were—and he was walking downtown, scarcely able to believe how wonderful
everything was. The sun was shining and the sky was
blue. Eleanor had to finish a few jobs, but her boss told
her just to work until three, and then she could take off.
Forrest was eager to buy her a ring right away, and he also
thought he would stop into the county courthouse to find
out what was needed in order to get a license. He stuck
his head into the jeweler's first to make sure they would
still be there at three, and having been assured solemnly
that they would be, he was then off to the courthouse.

When he burst into the office, three heads turned
to look at him. Sheriff Barnes was behind the counter
talking to the tax commissioner, and they both looked
up and returned to their conversation. The clerk, a
nondescript and disheveled man named Shandy shuf-
fled up to the counter.

"I wanted to ask about marriage licenses," Forrest
began.

"I am afraid you'll have to bring the young lady
with you," Shandy replied.

"Oh, I know that. I will be back with her in a few
hours. But I wanted to find out how much they cost. I
have go to the bank, and then the jeweler's and then
here. I just wanted to get the amount. I just got engaged
today. I just got engaged to Miss Eleanor Simpson."

"Oh, in that case, you will need two dollars. Bring
her with you, and we can take care of all that."

Forrest beamed at him, full of admiration for such a helpful clerk. "You know what?" he volunteered. The clerk Shandy shook his head. He didn't know what.

The sheriff had been acquainted with Mr. Sampson for years, and it slowly began to dawn on him that here he was at the counter, simply volunteering information. He had already spoken more words than the sheriff had ever heard him speak in the entire time he had known him. And it looked like he was going to say a lot more.

"You know what's funny?"

Shandy shook his head again. He didn't know what was funny.

"This world is not the way I thought it was. You could have knocked me down with . . . what is that saying again?"

"A feather?" Shandy asked.

"That's it! A feather. And you wouldn't even have to touch me with it. Just wave it, and over I would go. Blow me right down with a feather."

Shandy was interested, in spite of his general lethargic outlook, and the sheriff had stopped his conversation with the tax commissioner and now was simply staring. This was a man he did not recognize—but it was the same man, Forrest Sampson. He lived at the boardinghouse, and never spoke a word to *anybody*.

"She was waiting for me to speak my heart. She knew for *months*. Such a patient woman. A wise woman. I almost went into the laundry a few months ago— the night of that fire, remember?—to get it over with then and there. I was sure she would be very polite to me and icy cold, and I knew I couldn't take it. I walked back and forth in front of that laundry a bunch of times. She says she saw me, and felt so sorry for me. She is such a sweet woman."

At the phrase *the night of the fire*, the sheriff started. He waited patiently while Forrest finished telling the bemused Shandy about how he had discovered that the world was not such a cruel place after all. In fact, it was a lovely place. When Forrest finally finished, and made his way to the door, the sheriff muttered to the tax commissioner that he would be back shortly, maybe, and he followed Forrest out into the hallway.

Forrest heard the sheriff's boots on the tile as he was walking out, and so he turned and stopped. "Mr. Sampson," the sheriff said, coming up to him. "May I ask you a few questions please?"

"Sure enough." Forrest beamed. Anybody could ask him anything. He would give it to them too. Anything you wanted to know.

"You just said that you were walking back and forth in front of the laundry on the same night that fire happened. Did I hear you right?"

Forrest nodded cheerfully. "That's right. And all that torment for nothing. I could have just gone right in."

"Was this in the afternoon, or after dinner?"

"Oh, it was after dinner. The girls had a big pile to do, and Eleanor hadn't come back to the boarding-house for dinner, and so at first I was worried about it. I walked down there at first to make sure everything was all right. When I saw that it was all right, and that they were just working late, I walked back toward home. Then it occurred to me—meaning it came burning hot into my mind—that I could just go in and ask her. But I wasn't sure, so I walked past the laundry, up toward where I work."

The sheriff listened patiently.

"I did that a few times. She says she saw me walking back and forth."

"I see," the sheriff said. "In all your walking back and forth, did you happen to look across the street at the bank?"

"Oh, sure enough." Forrest grinned. Everything was making him happy. "I saw poor old Mr. Lambeth, working late again. He needs to find a woman. Once you find the right woman . . ." he began, but the sheriff put his hand up to stop him. Ordinarily the sheriff would have let him run on, but he was starting to get excited.

"Was Mr. Lambeth by himself?"

"Oh, yes. Real lonesome like. All the tellers had gone, and there was only one light on, the light in his office. I saw his silhouette, just one of them. All by himself. Yes. He works hard, that man does. But he needs a woman. I heard he made a try last year for Miss Savannah, what lives at our place. But he won't find a woman working late nights by himself at the bank, I can tell you that."

Sheriff Barnes was holding his excitement under, using both hands to keep it beneath the surface.

"Thanks very much, Mr. Sampson. And congratulations on your recent happiness. I may have some additional questions for you later, if you don't mind."

"Not at all," Forrest replied. "Happy to answer any questions you might have."

The sheriff walked down the hallway toward the other end of the courthouse, hoping that the judge was in his chambers. He needed to get a warrant for Lambeth's arrest. He was going to start with the fire and the murder both. Whatever the judge would give him. Shoot the moon. He now knew that Lambeth's alibi was a lie.

In the meantime, Forrest walked back over to the jewelers again to get an idea of how much rings would cost, and then he walked over to the bank to make his withdrawal.

Forrest walked into the bank, as happy and as garrulous as he had been at the courthouse. "I am going to buy an *engagement* ring!" he announced to Taylor, who was manning the cage. "She said *yes*."

"Well, congratulations," Taylor said. "Many blessings on the two of you. And about time, I might add."

"Hi, Mr. Lambeth!" Forrest waved over the top of Taylor's head. Alan Lambeth had appeared in the door of his office for a moment, and nodded curtly at Forrest. "Speak of the devil," Forrest added, "the sheriff and I were just talking about you."

Lambeth just grunted and disappeared back into his office. But he *had* noticed Forrest's comment. Why would they be talking about him?

***

A law clerk named Jensen was right outside the judge's office, filing papers in the massive wooden file cabinets that were to the right of the door going into the judge's office. He was kneeling on the floor, with a stack of folders next to him.

He was a small lizard of a man, with a look of cagey intelligence on his face, but of the kind that made him look sneaky. This was the man that had cooked up the easement scheme that Martin and Lambeth had been discussing some weeks before. He had burrowed into the woodwork of city government with just such purposes in mind, and thus far his career had been one of great success in that department.

The sheriff strode into the office and greeted Jensen politely, hiding his distaste successfully. "The judge in? Is he free?"

Jensen nodded, and so the sheriff walked up to the office door and tapped with his knuckles on the translucent pane. "Come in!" a voice boomed from the other side. The judge, Jeffrey Chalmers, was a big man in every sense of the word. He was three-hundred pounds, but tall and muscular, about six and a half feet, and he had bushy eyebrows, and a fierce mustache. When he had his robe on, and was up behind that mahogany bench, he was visibly formidable. Not all the defendants who came before him would plead guilty, but all of them *wanted* to.

He and the sheriff were good friends, which hadn't always been the case. They had clashed a few times early on, but their interests and frame of mind had coincided a couple of years before on a case that was almost as interesting as this one was. That had sealed their friendship, and they got along famously now.

"Come in, come in," Jensen heard him repeating, as the sheriff did so. And it was not hard for him to hear the conversation continuing, because the mechanism to the doorknob had just recently started malfunctioning—the judge had told him just yesterday to find somebody to look at it, which Jensen had done. In the meantime, since the locksmith was busy until the next week, the bolt remained off-kilter, and the door had to be pressed tightly to make it shut. This the sheriff did not do, not knowing the situation, and so the door swung slightly ajar, by two or three inches. Kneeling there by the door, Jensen could hear everything, clear as a bell.

"Well, judge," the sheriff said. "I have a warrant here in need of a signature."

"Who? Which case?"

The sheriff lowered his voice, but Jensen could still hear if he held his breath, which he did. "Lambeth. For the fire at the boardinghouse, and for the murder of Todd Martin."

The judge said something which Jensen didn't quite catch, but he could tell from the tone that the judge was surprised.

A moment passed, and then he heard, "You sure?" There was silence, and so Jensen guessed that the sheriff had nodded. Having heard more than enough,

Jensen thought it best if he were found on the other side of the room when the sheriff came out. He stood up, left the folders on the floor, and walked silently and briskly across the room to his desk. He pulled the right drawer open, and was assiduously looking in there for something when the sheriff appeared in the doorway again. Sheriff Barnes had not appeared to notice that the door had been ajar.

He disappeared down the hallway, and so Jensen walked to the large window that looked out over the street. In just a few minutes, the sheriff's large hat appeared below, which then turned left and the man under it walked purposefully down the street toward the sheriff's department. Jensen noted brief satisfaction that he was likely going to gather a few of his men before he went to arrest Lambeth.

Now it would be inaccurate to say that Jensen was motivated by any impulses of human kindness or decency, and would be far more accurate to say that he was concerned that if Lambeth were arrested, all sorts of connections might start appearing, all sorts of activities might come out. And in those activities, his name, the name of Jensen, was like to appear and reappear. It was in his best interest, and in the interest of his future legal career, that this not happen.

And so, thinking quickly, Jensen walked back to the judge's office and tapped on the glass himself. "Judge? I was going to step out to get myself a cherry coke—I can bring one back for you if you like." This is not something he always did, but he did it often enough that the judge would never think it was strange. And the soda fountain was just on the other side of the bank.

A few minutes later, Jensen was walking back toward the courthouse, a drink in each hand. There was no one ahead of him or behind him when he got to the bank, and so he walked briskly down the alley to the window that looked out from Lambeth's office. He looked in and saw that Lambeth was in there, fortunately by himself. He tapped on the window glass with one of the coke bottles.

Lambeth was already stewing about the comment that Forrest Sampson had made, and the sharp tap on the glass made him jump. He swiveled around in his chair, and his eyebrows shot up. Walking over to the window, he pulled it up and bent over with questions all over his face. Jensen? Tapping on the window?

Jensen whispered his news quickly, and didn't even stop to see if it registered. He walked back out to the street, looked both ways, and then stepped across the street to make his way back to the courthouse.

Although Jensen hadn't waited to see if it registered with Lambeth, it *had* registered with Lambeth. He walked across his office, picked up the pack he used when riding, pulled open some drawers and dropped a few things in it, including his gun and holster. He then went to another drawer for a wallet he kept in case of emergency. He cinched the pack tight, and walked out. He nodded curtly at Taylor. "I'll be back in about forty-five minutes." If the sheriff came to arrest him there at the bank, there was a chance that this would cool him down, make him wait for Lambeth to come back. Might buy some time, and time was at a premium.

Lambeth walked around the side of the bank, and headed straight for the stables. A rented horse could be ready in a few minutes, and with any kind of head start he had a good chance of making it to Lewiston, and from there out to the coast. He patted the wallet in his breast pocket. It was there, and full of his emergency cash. The sheriff wouldn't know which way to go—although his mostly likely options would be either north to Spokane or south to Lewiston. But Lambeth intended to take a back route, and thought he could shake them even if they guessed right.

But Taylor was a curious young man. And just like Jensen had walked over to the window to see which way the sheriff had gone, so Taylor walked to the back window of the bank to see which way that Lambeth had gone. He was able to keep him in sight for a block before he turned right, and that was almost certainly down toward the stables. There was nothing else down there. He asked Perkins to mind the store, and walked half a block after Lambeth, and then sat down in front of the shoe store on a bench they had. He hunched over so that it would be unlikely that Lambeth would recognize him, even if he looked over that way.

In about ten minutes, Lambeth appeared from the direction of the stables, turned south, and cantered off. He did not look to his right or left. Taylor got up and

ran back to the bank. He burst in the front door, and
Perkins, wide-eyed, said, "*What* is going on? You can't
just go off and leave me in charge like that."

Taylor was still standing by the front door, looking down the street. He, like Dr. Gritman, was a
reader of detective fiction, and his wheels had been
turning ever since he realized that Mr. Lambeth was
lying about Martin's hat. He was looking down the
street as though he was expecting the sheriff to come
any minute, and in this expectation, he was soon rewarded. In the distance, he saw Sheriff Barnes and
two of his men striding purposefully toward them.
Taylor held up his hand to shush Perkins, who was
still demanding an answer. "You'll hear everything in
just a minute."

When the sheriff came in, he looked back toward
Lambeth's office. "Mr. Lambeth in?"

Taylor shook his head. He and Perkins then said
"No" at the same time. "He should be back in about
half an hour," Perkins said helpfully.

"That's what he told us to say," Taylor added. "But
he headed toward the stables, and then rode out south.
No sense you waiting for him here. If it is urgent—as I
suspect it is—you could probably catch up with him if
you get saddled quick enough. But he left in a hurry."

The sheriff thanked Taylor, and the three men
turned to go. "One more thing," Taylor said. "If all this
is what I think it might be, a question or two might be
addressed at some point to Mr. Jensen, who works at

the courthouse. He popped out of the alley here, right before Mr. Lambeth decided to see the countryside."

The sheriff nodded, remembering how deliberate and careful Jensen was being as he had left the judge's office.

Half an hour later, the sheriff and his men were on the road, but sitting stationary on their horses. Two cars were parked by the side of the road. A faint pathway led off to the left. One of the sheriff's men dismounted and walked slowly up the path a few feet.

"Well, should we go straight on to Lewiston? Or take this path? Or split up and do both?" the sheriff asked.

The man who had dismounted was examining the ground. "Two sets of prints," he said. "A gent's and a lady's. Probably not together. The lady came first—several of his prints are on top of hers." He began to walk on either side of the path, alongside the road. About five feet to the south, he stopped again. "And a horse went up this way, avoiding the dust of the path. Recent."

"Well, there's our answer," the sheriff said.

APOCALYPSE

De-noue-ment, n. the final resolution or clarification
of a dramatic or narrative plot
THE AMERICAN HERITAGE DICTIONARY

Savannah had parked the car by the highway, down at a turnout in a small valley, and had walked up to her spot. There was a clustered spinney of trees near the top, and she stood on the south side of those trees, looking off across the undulating hills. It was a clear day and she wished she could see the Seven Devils, far off to the south. But that was not possible. She had come up here to pray and cry, as she usually did on these visits, but this time strangely found herself unable to do either. So she just stood quietly, watching clouds tumble in the south and late autumn approach stealthily from the west.

Thomas had borrowed Mr. Felton's car, at the strong insistence of Mr. Felton. He had followed Savannah out of town about a half hour later, and when he saw her car parked, he pulled over as well, guessed where she must have walked, and followed the deer trail up. After about fifteen minutes of walking, he saw her standing at the top of the hill, outlined against the sky.

Savannah saw him about the same time that he saw her. She had been startled when she first recognized him, but by the time he was close enough to see her face, she had regained her composure. "Pastor Thomas . . . what brings you here?"

He had taken off his hat to speak, and hesitated for a moment. For just a moment. "Well, Savannah, there is no sense drawing this out. This is what we agreed to at the banquet. I wanted to come up here and declare my love to you. I wanted to ask you to be my wife."

She had been half expecting this, part of her dreading it, and part of her longing for it. She opened her mouth, and then closed it abruptly. "I am flattered . . . and I am honored. I truly am. But I am not worthy. I am afraid I could not be a minister's wife. I . . . I am afraid it is quite impossible."

Thomas took a step closer. "May I press my suit . . .?" he began. She held up her hand in a way that tremblingly asked him to not come any closer.

"Pastor Thomas, you are tormenting me. I am torn between what I need to say to you as my suitor, as I suppose this declaration now makes you, and what I must say to you as my pastor."

Thomas stopped as she requested and stood quietly, saying nothing.

Savannah licked her lips, trying to find her courage. She had no idea where it had gone. After a moment she spoke again, trying to speak without it, and praying to God that her voice wouldn't quaver. It almost didn't.

"If I tell you, you will quite understand why I am turning aside attentions that would otherwise . . . that would otherwise be quite welcome. But if I tell you, I am afraid you will despise me, and I don't know what I could do. I could not bear it."

Thomas remained still. "You may tell me. I will not despise you, regardless of what it is. I *could* not despise you."

Savannah paused again for a moment, fatally decided, and then began. "Five years ago, after my parents had died of the influenza, I came west. I was quite headstrong, full of my dreams, vain and conceited dreams, which is just another way of saying I was very full of myself. Looking back, and thoroughly ashamed of myself, I can see that I was dazzled by my own daydreams. All of those dreams were dashed in rapid succession, one after another, and I found myself with very little money, no prospects, and on a train heading northwest from Chicago. They were pitiful dreams, really, to be destroyed so easily, but they had been my dreams, and I was very sad about it."

"Go on," Thomas said gently.

"The fact that my dreams had all been dashed—no one wanted to hear me sing, no one wanted to buy the songs I had written, no one wanted to hire me to play piano for their productions—did not mean that my conviction that I had a *right* to such dreams had been dashed. The dreams were in pieces, but I was egotistically very angry about it. My resentment was not in pieces. That resentment was whole and entire. You can see, perhaps, that I have done a great deal of thinking about all of this."

She stopped, and Thomas waited patiently. "There was a woman on the train who was very kind to me. She saw immediately the straits I was in, and invited me to stay with her in . . . in Milwaukee. She . . . she was a madam, and owned a house . . . a house of ill repute. I blush to say it, but I do want to say she was very kind to me."

Thomas still said nothing, and she looked at him sharply. "You see now why I cannot accept you? That should be quite enough for a proper suitor, who may guess the rest of the story. But having said so much, I must now tell you the rest of it as my pastor. May I?"

"You may," Thomas said. "But I do need to say one thing about all this first. I have no intention of being one of those domineering pastors who weasels secrets out of people as a way of controlling them . . . but if knowing something that you want to tell me would be a help to you, then I do want to be your pastor."

She nodded in appreciation, and briefly wondered why he didn't look more troubled at what was obviously coming, but quickly resumed before she lost her nerve.

"After a week with her, I told her that I could not accept her charity any longer, and that I needed to pay her. I . . . I . . . I offered to become one of her girls. I did this in part because I needed the money desperately, which I did . . . but there were other factors also. I mentioned that my plans were all of them wrecked, and because I was a very conceited and proud young woman, I was hungry for something, anything, that would flatter me. And in the honesty of confessing to a pastor I must tell you this part also. I was fascinated by what was happening in the house, and by her very real kindness to me, which is not something I would have guessed, and I felt drawn to all of that. I blush to tell you this part also, but it was a real part of my sin. I did not know the Lord then, but that doesn't make it any the less sinful, or any less of a disgrace."

Thomas nodded, as if to invite her to continue. He looked grave, but he still did not look troubled. She wondered why he wasn't looking more troubled.

"After some argument, she reluctantly agreed to my request. She did not want me to do it at all for some reason. But I prevailed, and I joined the line-up of girls that evening. It was a Tuesday evening, I recall. I was picked out of the line, and went up to my room where the customer was to join me a short time later. I was full of terror and desire both, and, as soon as it was over, all of the terror and all of the desire was immediately replaced by nothing but remorse. I have no idea where the remorse all came from, but I have never felt so terrible in all my days. Nothing but remorse in every direction. I was not surprised by the fact of it, for I had expected some, but I did not know what to do with the depth and extent of it. Early next morning I packed my bags, gave my dear friend the money I owed her, which she did not want to take, but I insisted, and went to the train station. I wanted to head farther west, but whatever direction I went, I needed to depart from there. My heart was sick, and I did not know why it was sick."

She stopped again for a moment, until Thomas quietly said, "Go on."

"At the next stop the conductor invited us to stretch our legs for a few hours, and so I walked back and forth on the road on the far side of the train station. I don't even remember the name of the town. There was a preacher there, though, standing on the end of a watering trough outside a saloon. He did not have much of the love of God about him, he looked like nothing on earth, and he was *full* of hatred for sin. But for whatever reason, his words spoke to me, I called upon the Lord, and was saved on the spot. I don't know how I even knew what that was, but I nevertheless knew what it was. When I got back on the train, I was rejoicing and traveled in that state of joy until I got to Spokane. And as it happened, the day before we reached Spokane, I struck up a conversation with a man who happened to be the mayor—the previous mayor—here in Paradise Valley. He told me there was an opening here to teach school, and that he had the authority to make that hire. I applied for the position with him, he interviewed me right there on the train and hired me. I got off the train in Spokane, came down here, and have been here ever since. You see, then, that I am one of your more needy parishioners, a parishioner with quite a lurid past. I am forgiven, and I do know that, but sin still has consequences. I trust that you have seen immediately why I could not be a respected minister's wife with such a terrible secret in my past."

"Who was the man?" Thomas asked.

"I don't know," Savannah replied. "He was a young man, and seemed nice enough. He thanked me when he left. But the room was too dark to see him clearly . . . I had made quite sure of that. The lamps were all dimmed."

"And from your story, I am assuming there was no child?"

"No, there was not, for which fact I have thanked the Lord many times. *Many* times."

Thomas, despite what she had said earlier, took a step closer. "Please let me be sure that I have heard you correctly. You believe that you could not become my wife because of this secret from your past. Five years ago, you worked for one night in a bordello, and you were with one man. Is that correct?"

"That is correct." But she also shook her head a little impatiently and her eyes flashed. "And also very *obvious*."

"And there is nothing I could say that could persuade you to think otherwise?"

"Nothing. And I would ask you again to please not torment me."

"But I believe that I could say something that would change everything for you. Not for me. For you."

She was expecting words to that effect, but something in his tone of voice brought her up sharply. "I don't know what you . . . what do you mean?"

"I mean," Thomas said, looking at her evenly, "that *I* was that man."

Savannah sat down suddenly on a fallen tree that was right next to her. It was fortunate that it was there because she would have sat down regardless. She had turned white, and was staring silently at Thomas.

"What!? Did . . . did I hear you correctly?"

"Yes, you heard me correctly. I was the man who was with you in Milwaukee that night. You have only been with one man in your life, and his name was Thomas Goforth."

Savannah opened her mouth and then closed it again. She had absolutely no idea what to say or do.

"May I explain further?" Thomas asked. "I owe you an explanation in many ways."

She nodded silently. Some of the color had come back into her face, but once it started to come back it returned with a vengeance, and she flushed crimson. She was beyond humiliated. She was mortified. A number of contrary emotions, all of them bad, were jumbling around inside her. She had slept with her *pastor*. Pastor Thomas knew about it. He had known for months. He had to have known during *all* their conversations . . .

"You will no doubt be too gracious to ask me to prove it, but it will be simple enough for me to supply a few details. It was in mid-August, the madam's last name was Steubens, and the house was about three blocks from the train station. And as I was leaving your room, I heard you sob."

Savannah nodded. "Yes. Go on," she said, about to sob again.

"My parents had both died at our home in Virginia, like yours, also of the Spanish flu. I had been brought up in a believing home, but one that was more influenced by the new thought from Germany than it should have been. My parents were not really affected by any of that, but they should have been more suspicious of what it might do to someone like me. After they died, I attended seminary for a year, in which time I completely lost my faith, helped along by Mr. Schleiermacher, and I left the seminary in disgust. I decided to come west in order to make my fortune, or find out what I was supposed to be doing instead of making a fortune. I had a little money from my parents, with the rest to be paid out later when the estate was settled. I was also hungry for adventure of some kind. I had a copy of Mr. Darwin's book with me, and spent a lot of time thinking through the implications of all of that. By the time I arrived in Milwaukee, I was a complete nihilist, or so I thought. But even though I now believed myself to be nothing more than a ganglion of nerves, I still had a bad case of the lonesomes. I determined that a visit to . . . to Madam Steubens's house . . . would help set my jangled nerves straight. And besides, it would be my definitive declaration of independence from my parents' faith, which I was by this point eager to do. And nothing was supposed to matter anyway."

"When did you recognize me? When you got here to Paradise, I mean?"

"Oh, I knew straight away. I had spent some time in the saloon beforehand studying all of you girls. I had memorized your face, and had asked for you particularly. So you can imagine my sensations that first Sunday here when I ascended the pulpit, looked out, and saw you sitting there in the third row. I can't imagine what listening to that sermon must have been like."

"Go on," Savannah said, smiling slightly. It had been an interesting sermon, but he had recovered nicely by the second Sunday. Her emotions were still in a state of high conflict, elbowing each other. Suddenly, without warning, anger was in the front of the others again, and she found herself speaking fiercely. "Why didn't you tell me right away? To leave me not knowing, and you knowing . . . simply *unbearable*."

"I almost did tell you. I certainly wanted to. In fact, I was going to tell you several times. But each time, after reflecting on it overnight, I decided that I needed to win your trust first. If I had told you straight away, all you would have known is that your new minister was a thundering hypocrite, and that the leading town hypocrite knew about your unhappy secret. I decided that if I told you right away, you would simply have disappeared again."

That stopped her anger short because it was completely true. She would have been gone the next morning. She wanted to be gone now. "Go on," she said again.

"I don't know that my decision was the wisest, but it was made with your best interests in mind. The thing had been done, and nothing to be done about it. I was now your pastor, and nothing to be done about that either. I decided that when I told you—and I always knew that I would do so at some point—it should be when you knew me well enough to . . . not to bolt."

Savannah stood up again, slowly, her hand covering her mouth. "Pastor Thomas," she said, "I don't know if you can know . . . how awful this is. This is not a revelation, this is an *apocalypse*."

"Savannah, I know that we feel our humiliation differently, you as a woman and I as a man. I cannot pretend to know how you feel. But I felt and feel as one who should have been protecting you, and behaved rather as someone you needed to be protected from. And that is why I wanted to know you well enough to be able to ask you to hear the entire story. And I decided within days of meeting you again that these two things were consistent with each other—humiliation for what I did to you, and delight in being with you again. Those are not contradictory."

She was quiet for another moment, and then asked, "What was the rest of your story?"

"As I was leaving your room in Milwaukee, as I said, I heard you sob. It cut my heart clean in two, for reasons I did not understand. I was a very bad nihilist, and there is nothing worse than a pathetic, milksop nihilist. I was wounded in the conscience, and I was very angry with myself for still having a conscience. My philosophical amateurism had banished my conscience, and then all my childhood Sunday School lessons, not to mention the reproachful face of my departed mother, brought my conscience back to life again, acting as though it had never even been gone. After my conscience rose from the dead, it wasn't even acting sick. I staggered downstairs, walked out into the street, and went back to my room, having a silent but high-pitched argument with myself. I got no sleep that night, and by noon the next day, I had decided to come back to the house to speak with you for a moment and beg your pardon. I should have begged your forgiveness, but I didn't know what that was yet. When I got there, Madam Steubens told me you were gone—she was very kind to me also. She told me that it was your first time. She had no idea what direction you had gone."

"I came directly here," Savannah said.

"Yes . . . I see that. I know that now." Thomas stopped. "May I tell you the rest?"

"Please." Savannah had recovered some of her equilibrium, and had realized mentally that Pastor Thomas was entailed in that sin, the same sin, every bit as much as she was, but still his sin had no emotional reality for her, not the way her own had. He had done such a fine job of establishing his moral authority in her life over the past months that she had no shelf on which to place this new information.

"I tried to guess what direction you had gone, guessed wrong, selecting St. Louis for some reason, and took the train there, detesting myself the entire way. I spent two days walking around aimlessly. After those two fruitless days, the next morning happened to be Sunday, and I was walking by a small Baptist chapel and heard them singing inside. I stepped inside, and sat down in the back row. The preacher was a blind man, but he must have known I was there somehow, and an angel must have told him right where I was sitting. He ran at least three homiletical spears straight through me. They gave an invitation, but I didn't go down. I slipped outside instead, and went straight to the train station, bleeding all the way. I purchased a ticket home, and was converted, I think, somewhere in Ohio."

"What did you do when you got home?"

"There were a few things remaining to be done, so I finished putting my parents' affairs in order, decided to go to Princeton Seminary—I had heard that they still believed in God there—and so it was that I finished my studies. There wasn't a day that I didn't think of you, there wasn't a day when I didn't pray for you. I told one man there my story—Professor Warfield was a fine Christian man. Shortly before he died, he told me to surrender it all to the Lord, finish my studies, stand for ordination at presbytery, and then find a church out west. He told me not to search for you, but to just ask God to bring you. He suggested that I wait on the Lord for that grace, for that gift, for at least three years. But there you were the first Sunday."

Savannah looked down at her hands. They were still trembling. "Well, you were right. You have told me something I could never have anticipated."

"I also wanted to tell you this. Despite my struggles and unbelief, my upbringing had a strong hold on me, and because of that, you were the first woman I was ever with. And there were certainly no women after. And so when I ask for your hand, I want you to know that I know what I am doing. I say that in part so that you will remember that I am still asking for your hand, and am renewing my request. This is awkward, I know."

Savannah started to answer, but then halted. After a moment she started up again. "We are certainly speaking frankly with each other, are we not? May I ask you a direct question . . . I am already so humiliated that I don't think that I could say anything to make that worse, but just because I am mortified I don't want to seem ungrateful or unkind."

"Please ask me anything you wish."

"So you have known about me since you arrived. I had no notion about you. I knew that you were likely pursuing me, but with my secret, I knew that I could not possibly become any minister's wife, still less the wife of a minister as gifted and godly as . . . as you plainly are. That is why I avoided you, escaped you in various ways, and was sometimes very rude to you. I am very sorry for all of that, by the way."

Thomas shook his head. "Please don't apologize. Within a very short time, I knew what a sincere Christian you were. I knew about the two of us, and it was very clear that you had not recognized me. And I also knew that this episode in your past was quite likely why you were avoiding my attentions. But what is your question?"

"Are you asking for my hand as a way of making restitution? Trying to put everything back in its place, making everything tidy and right again? Or is . . . there anything more, anything else? I don't want to feel like you are doing the same kind of thing as coming back later to pay someone for a stolen mule."

Thomas looked at the ground for a moment. "In one way, that is a hard question to answer. I do know what you are asking. And I believe that these are circumstances where this kind of restitution through marriage could be appropriate, provided both parties were now Christian, and both willing. And honestly that was in my mind for the first week or so after I recognized you. But ever since the affair of the potato salad at the church picnic, I have been desperately, hopelessly, in love with you. If there had been no Milwaukee, I would still be standing right here. I would have been standing here sooner."

Savannah smiled a second time, blushing slightly. "The potato salad?"

"Yes. So that is my plea. I love you and want to be with you. But if you show any reluctance, I would be willing to bring in the stolen mule argument as additional support for my case. I will enlist any support that might be effective."

Savannah took a deep breath, stood up, and extended both her hands toward him, palms down. "No," she said, "no reluctance. Deep embarrassment, and deeper humiliation, but no reluctance."

That was all Thomas needed, all he was waiting for, and so he stepped quickly up to her, ignoring her arms and hands, embraced her, and kissed her firmly, warmly, completely. After a moment he stepped back, and then took her hands in his. "Well then," he said.

RELEASE

Thy law commands me to be blessed;
My duty is my interest.

SAMUEL DAVIES

Thomas and Savannah stood together for a number of minutes, saying nothing. Thomas just held her in his embrace, and Savannah was simply willing to be held. He wasn't sure if she were crying. After a time, he stepped back and saw that she had been.

"Are you ready to go?" he asked. "We *should* go," he added. Savannah nodded her head in agreement.

They both turned down the hill, and Thomas continued speaking, a little awkwardly, trying to accommodate her silence. "It is unfortunate that we will have

to part so soon, but lamentably we do have two borrowed cars down by the highway. But we can be together until then. And because we are just a few miles
from town, we can be together again shortly after. Not
trying to be jocular. Just trying." She smiled gamely.

And with that Thomas presented his right arm to
Savannah, and she took it. She also took great pleasure
in feeling how solid his upper arm was. This was no
effete clergyman.

They walked silently for a space. "You are being
very quiet," Thomas eventually said.

"I have no words," Savannah said. "I alternate between ecstasy and humiliation, and my vocabulary is
insufficiently flexible."

Thomas reached around her shoulders, squeezed
her gently, and then presented his arm to her once
more. She took it again.

Savannah continued, "It does occur to me to say
something fitting and appropriate when I am in the
grip of each sentiment, but the emotions change so
rapidly that I do not trust myself to end any given sentence in the same frame of mind as when I began it. So
perhaps my silence is not unwise."

"If it helps," Thomas said, "I went through my
own version of the same kind of thing months ago,
in the weeks after I recognized you. But I had the advantage of being able to stay quiet about it. I did not
have to talk to you—or deal with anybody else—in the
midst of what I was feeling. I did punch my pillow a
few times . . . but the pillow didn't seem to care. And I

also had an advantage in the fact that I had been praying that I would sometime meet you. Still, it was quite
a shock when I *did*."

"That just provides me with another round of con-
flicts. It helps a great deal, and it doesn't help at all."
Savannah laughed at herself, and felt her cheek with
the back of her hand. It was still hot. "You are going to
have to be patient with me."

"I will be patient. I understand."

She resumed after a moment. "And you were always so confident around me . . . why would you
punch a pillow?"

"It is true that I was confident whenever I was with
you. You make me want to stand up straight, and so
I always do. But when you weren't there . . . believe
me, I had more than a few moments of black despair.
And if anything is guaranteed to interfere with sermon
preparation, it is black despair."

Savannah smiled to herself, a little gamely, but it was
a real smile. She was wrestling to keep it a real smile.
It had only been fifteen minutes, and she had already
thought of breaking their engagement two or three
times. But *that* didn't make sense. The problem was that
staying engaged didn't seem to make sense either.

They were about halfway down the hill at this
point, and came to a long grove of tamaracks, with the
path winding down through the center of it. Walking
into the shade, they began talking more quietly, as
though to honor the informal and murmuring sanctity
of the green cathedral. They were not very far into the

grove when Thomas suddenly stopped. "Hooves," he said, and Savannah stopped alongside him.

They stood silently for a moment, waiting to see who it would be. There was a small gulch that crossed the path just up ahead of them, and Thomas could see the hat of the rider just before he came up over the crest of it. That gave him a fleeting warning, and so he took a step forward so that he could jump in front of Savannah if he needed to. It was going to be Lambeth. It was.

As he came over the rise, he was looking backward over his right shoulder, as though he were being pursued, as in fact he was. When he turned forward in his saddle, he was startled to see Thomas and Savannah, standing there in the middle of his path. He reined his horse in quickly.

His face had been full of concern over the posse on his trail—for he knew there *had* to be a posse on his trail—but that concern vanished, and instantly a sneer replaced it. "Well, well," he said, pulling out a revolver. "Are we lovebirds now?" He had been seething over that prospect for weeks now, but it was no less galling when he saw it right before him.

He nudged his horse, and it came slowly forward. His revolver was pointed directly at Thomas's forehead. At the same time, it was clear that he knew he didn't have much time to spare, and that he was worried about it. He kept turning sideways in his saddle, so as to listen for horses behind him.

He was also calculating furiously. He had fled Paradise when Jensen from the courthouse had told him there was going to be a warrant out for his arrest for the murder of Todd Martin, and possibly for the arson death of Mrs. Warner. For all the obvious reasons, Lambeth decided immediately to flee. He thought he could get away, over the ridge and down to the river by a back way, a way he had used often when hunting. From the river he thought he could get to Portland, and then book passage down to Mexico. He didn't think that a lot of resources would be devoted to pursuing him.

But this! If he did what he now had both the opportunity and inclination to do, which was to have his full vengeance on both Thomas and Savannah, and to deny them any future happiness together, it might be fully worth it. And depending on how much time he thought he had, he wouldn't have to shoot her right away . . . the posse would no doubt be slowed down by the discovery of the bodies, and that would be most helpful, but he also knew the pursuit after that point would be savage and relentless. A murdered minister and a beautiful young woman would be a sensational crime, and nobody would rest until they found him. They might even want to track him down in Mexico. His pragmatic intelligence, which was considerable, told him to just spur his horse past them and be on his way. He could settle for an insult or two as he rode past.

But then Lambeth felt that clammy spirit of envy descend on him, a spirit he had known his entire life — though it had never been so weighty as it was at this moment. Never this heavy. He thought he was making up his mind, though it was actually his mind having something else entirely done to it. Something that felt both dark green and black seemed to have him by the throat. He was breathing with some difficulty. Nevertheless, he urged his horse a few feet closer.

"Well, I would usually want to make a fine speech here, but I must also allow that I don't really have time for it. Let's just say that precious in the sight of the Lord is the death of his saints."

With that, he pulled the hammer back on his revolver and started to take proper aim.

Just as thick suffocating envy had descended upon Lambeth, so in that same moment an equally thick and equally suffocating despair descended upon Thomas. He had never known such exultation as the moment when Savannah had accepted him, and here, now, right at the moment of fruition, God was apparently knocking it out of his hand out of spite.

His most immediate sensation was that of time slowing down, that time in which he assumed people were supposed to see their lives pass before them. But that is not how he found himself spending his slowed down experience of time. It was as though there were three of him, and they were all arguing with one another. One of him was frustrated that with all the extra time to think, he was still not able to think about how to counter Lambeth. The revolver was still pointed at his head, and time slowing down just meant he had a longer time to observe Lambeth exult in his victory over him. The second Thomas was simply raging against God. The third Thomas was lecturing the second Thomas, explaining to him that his position was theologically and philosophically untenable and incoherent. But the second Thomas was the one who was making all the noise.

Prior to his conversion, Thomas had been the kind of unbeliever who resented the God he did not believe was there. He resented that this God did not exist, He resented that this non-existent God had created such a world as this one plainly was, He resented that God had created him without his permission, and he resented that he had no God to resent. His conversion had been such that all of these resentments had just fallen away from him in the course of a few minutes. His deliverance from "all that" had been complete.

But *now*, for God to give him this woman, and then to take her away from him just a few minutes later, seemed to him to be petty and vindictive on a cosmic scale. All the old resentments flooded back—unbeknown to him, the same fetid cloud that was driving Lambeth to murder him out of envy was the same miasma that fell upon Thomas like an oppressive weight. The two men both had the same acrid taste in their spiritual mouths. One was going to murder out of resentment and the other was going to be murdered in resentment.

The difference was that Thomas was fighting it, and was fully aware of how ludicrous it was to be representing old apologetics lectures to himself on the very threshold of dying. Why couldn't he use this mental energy to figure out what to do about getting shot? But instead he was busy meeting the challenge presented by this old Adam who had apparently arisen out of nowhere. "What standard do you have to bring a charge against God?" he said. "What court shall you arraign him in?" This old Adam seemed to him to present a much graver threat than Lambeth was presenting to him.

But just as Lambeth wasn't going anywhere, so also the second angry Thomas didn't seem to be going anywhere.

Years of praying, years of longing, years of hope deferred. Then after all that time, he accepted a call to a church that he knew nothing about, and the only reason for doing it was the fact that it was located in the Pacific Northwest. And then, right on the first Sunday, there she was, seated in his church, and he was her pastor. And she was a Christian, which he had no right to expect. She was lovelier than anything he had ever seen in his life, and it seemed to him then that God was simply giving him a gift. But no, God was actually giving him a gift for about twenty minutes. For his mercy endures *forever*. Thomas threw his charges against the divine goodness across his mind savagely.

The third Thomas stared back at himself with astonishment. "I have no intention of dying in a state of impudent rebellion. This all seems hopeless, but how is it not an argument the other way? Why do we not trust God to finish what He began? The people of Israel were delivered on the banks of the Red Sea. Abraham was spared from having to kill his son when the knife was in his right hand, and raised above his head. David had numerous hairbreadth escapes in the wilderness with Saul in pursuit. God plainly loves cliffhangers, and that is what this most certainly is."

And the first Thomas was staring at the revolver, watching Lambeth's thumb pulling the hammer back. He was thinking furiously and could think of absolutely nothing. He was praying desperately, and no answers were forthcoming. He was preparing to leap, knowing that whatever direction he might decide to leap, it would all be in vain.

The second Thomas was brute force silenced, and fell down dead. The third Thomas gave glory to God, and the first Thomas tensed and braced.

And that is when Savannah decided to pop open her parasol in the horse's face. She thought it would be an effective and helpful thing to do, but the results were far, far beyond her expectations. That Appaloosa was a skittish one to begin with, and had just had a rattlesnake scare the day before, and the parasol was very white, very bright, and made a most satisfactory popping noise when she thrust it open as quickly as she did. The horse had already been having a difficult week, and now reared up, bucking violently. Lambeth was a good horseman, but he could have been a rodeo champion for all that it mattered. He flew in one direction, and his revolver flew in the other. The gun hit a rock where it went off as it struck, the sound echoing through the trees.

Thomas dashed forward and pounced on Lambeth just a second after he landed. The horse was off the path to the right, crashing through the bracken. Savannah darted over to the revolver, picked it up, and walked deliberately back toward where the two men were struggling. She stopped about ten yards away from them. She saw right away that she could be no help to Thomas if she came in any closer, and she could use the gun appropriately as necessary if she stayed where she was.

Lambeth was a powerful man, and had managed in a strong lurch to throw Thomas off him. He clambered to his feet and looked around frantically for his revolver. Savannah held it up for him pleasantly, pointing it toward the sky. But Lambeth's attentions were immediately pulled back away from Savannah as a powerful right cross from Thomas staggered him. He had made yet another mistake in throwing Thomas off him.

Thomas was a very poor wrestler, and had even been cut from the team at Princeton, but he had been a magnificent boxer. In their periodic conversations, the two respective coaches had sometimes remarked on the disparity. Very curious, they both found it.

Another right rattled Lambeth, and he shook his head in a slow and muddled way. He tried ineffectively to get his hands up in a way that could somehow stop Thomas. He had taken some haymaker swings at Thomas, but most were parried quite easily.

Seconds later, a posse of five men—the sheriff had picked up two extra when they were scrambling for

their horses—came up over the crest in the path, hur-
ried on in their pursuit by the earlier gunshot. All of
them stopped their horses in amazement. Thomas was
by this point scientifically dismantling Lambeth who,
despite all his strength, could not figure out any way to
stop the minister's fists.

"Is that our *pastor*?" one of the men asked. Another of the men, a Baptist and a good friend of Taylor's,
shook his head slowly. He had no category for this.

Savannah said *yes* proudly. Her deep humiliation
was gone, and as soon as it was gone Lambeth toppled
over, like a tree falling down a steep slope. The sheriff
leading the posse swung down from his horse instantly, getting out his handcuffs.

Her humiliation had disappeared. Vanished. She
had known she was forgiven before, and had felt the
reality of that forgiveness many times. She had had
countless conversations with herself about it, and had
worked through it many times. If she had conceived a
child, she could have been just as completely forgiven
as she knew herself to be. But being forgiven wouldn't
have made the child disappear. Sin has consequences,
and even forgiven sin also has its forgiven but real consequences. Her consequences were not in a child, but
rather in what it did, as she viewed it, to her marriage
prospects. Since she had become a Christian, she had
developed very high views of the married state and
of what kind of man she would want for a husband.
And she knew the kind of man that she wanted and
needed would have to be told . . . and there was the

consequence. The kind of man she would need would
need—she was convinced—a woman not at all like
her. She would need him, but he would not need her.

And this unexpected conversation with Thomas
had brought the full *weight* of her secret back to her—
and while his confession and proposal had checkmat-
ed that weight, it had still been there. And her pride
was still there. That is what she meant by alternating
between ecstasy and humiliation.

But now . . . this sudden freedom when Lambeth
fell was not part of that alternating pendulum. The
weight was gone and gone forever. She didn't know
how she knew that it was gone forever, but she just
knew. She felt very much like how she had felt when
she had been converted, but it was in an entirely different place. This freedom was elsewhere, *everywhere* else.

Her future husband was standing over Lambeth
now, and Savannah exulted. You could not tell it by
looking at her, but she was soaring. Her man was a
sinner, just like she was, and the sovereign God had
picked up all of their broken pieces and assembled
them into an unbelievable glory. Her man was a *sinner*, and yet he was standing over his adversary victo-
rious. God gives victory to men who do not deserve
it. Her man was her man, and would never belong
to another. She would never belong to another, and
she never *had* belonged to another. She thought that
when she got home that evening she would have to
compose a hymn to sovereign grace, or burst in the
trying. No humiliation.

God was God. She marveled at His wisdom and knew that she had not gotten off on a technicality. She had gotten off because she was in the hands of a God who was infinitely wise. Her deliverance was not her doing. She could just as easily have been with some other man. She could just as easily have been the instrument of destroying some poor other woman's happiness, leaving *her* with an unfaithful man. So she had sinned in just the ways she had always known that she had sinned. She had known forgiveness for that sin, but what this release amounted to was a crushing knowledge of what *God* is like. It had little to do with what she was like. She had always known of her sin, and of forgiveness. She had known that she needed forgiveness, and she knew that God forgave. She had tasted grace, and knew that she had.

But she had not always known that when the apostle had said His ways are past all finding out, that this meant that His wisdom was an infinite series of labyrinthine infinities, each one more complex than the last one. And He used *all* of this wisdom when He cared for His people. He cared for *her*. He had tied this intricate plot together for her.

She had been a whore; she was to be a virgin bride. She was a Magdalene, and now she felt like she knew what it was like to be the first at the empty tomb. She had been wise in her own conceits, and now she felt all those conceits blowing like straws in a tornado. She was the straw, in a hurricane of grace. She no longer cared about trying to keep inventory on her straws as they flew by her. God spoke from the whirlwind, and they were words of wisdom and kindness and grace, and Savannah laughed out loud.

She was Hannah and had gotten the victory over her adversary. She was the woman who had thrown a millstone off the tower, and Abimelech lay broken at the bottom. The serpent had always had a special distaste for women, and she had had vengeance on her enemy. She was Jael, wife of Heber, and she had done it with a parasol.

Savannah walked over to a deputy and handed him the revolver. He had no idea how loudly her heart was singing. She turned toward Thomas, who was carefully brushing off his coat, ran toward him, and buried herself in his chest. "Hello?" said two of the sheriff's men, and one of them finished with, "What's all this?" Thomas just held her without speaking for long minutes.

When she finally pulled back, she finished brushing him off, and then jumped slightly, startled because she saw Thomas's right eye. In the entire fight, Lambeth had only landed once, but it had been a good one. "Oh, dear," Savannah said, touching the edge of it gingerly. "That is going to be a garish one. I am not sure a pastor should look like such a rogue."

Thomas grinned. "I will have to work it into a sermon illustration somehow." His face darkened. "Although I hope this doesn't mean we have to postpone the wedding." He touched his eye gingerly.

"We will postpone nothing. It will give the event an extra flare."

"Then I am entirely content," he said.

"You . . . you are quite a boxer, I can see."

"And you were magnificent with that parasol. I don't mind saying that I was thinking pretty hard at just that moment, and coming up with mostly nothing. That was one of the most elegant and timely things I think I have ever seen." Thomas chuckled, rejoicing at the story he now had for his grandchildren. His inner turmoil had vanished, just like it had never been. He knew God was good, he knew that He was fond of cliffhangers, and he had a story of deliverance that he would never tire of telling himself.

The sheriff had come up just then to ask them some official questions about what had happened, and this seemed like a good way into a proper accounting of things. "Parasol?" he asked.

They told *him* the whole story. One of the sheriff's men had gone off to get the runaway horse, and he arrived back on the trail with the Appaloosa in question just as they were finishing up their account. The sheriff's eyes widened. "*That's* the horse you popped your parasol on? That poor hoss . . . that snake yesterday, and another one today." He glanced at Lambeth when he said this.

Two of the sheriff's men got Lambeth up on a horse with some difficulty—he being sullen and uncooperative—and they headed back down toward the highway, one leading the horse and the other riding behind with his hand on his revolver. Thomas had an idea, and asked the sheriff if one of his other two men could drive Mr. Felton's car back to town so that he and Savannah could take Mrs. Fuller's car back together. The sheriff cheerfully agreed. He had gotten his man, and was feeling very agreeable about everything.

They all made it down to the road with no difficulty. The sheriff, his prisoner, and three men headed north toward town. Thomas spent a few minutes explaining his car to the young man who was to drive it back. He—William—seemed to know what he needed to know about driving, but he was still quivering with excitement. "*Slow,* mind you," Thomas said. "First, it is a borrowed car. And especially go slow when you go past the horses. You don't want to spook them and be the occasion for the prisoner getting away. " That was about the only thing Thomas could have said to calm him down, because the sheriff was truly agreeable when he was agreeable, but he was a fierce one when he wasn't.

Thomas and Savannah watched carefully as the car inched away from them and toward the disappearing posse at about ten miles per hour.

Thomas then turned and opened the driver's side door for Savannah. Her eyebrows went up. "Mrs. Fuller's car," he explained. "We want to be most conscientious. I didn't borrow it, and don't know that I have her blessing to drive it."

Savannah shrugged, and started to get in. She stopped suddenly, startled, when Thomas slapped at his breast pocket, and exclaimed, "Why, if I haven't gone and left out a key element!"

Her eyes were wide. "What? What!"

"The ring," he said. "In all our excitement, I neglected to give you the ring." He was fishing out a small box, a box that looked as though it had been through a great deal, which it had.

Savannah looked down at the box, and then gasped. "McCall's Jewelry? That's in Spokane, right next to the Davenport!" Her excitement dampened somewhat. "That poor little box . . ."

Thomas looked pleased with himself. "That's where I was the night of the ball. I had just come from there when I interrupted Mr. Watkins' . . . um . . . attempts to insinuate himself into your good graces. I had picked out the ring a week or two before, and just had to pick it up. When I saw that Mr. Watkins was losing ground with you by the minute I thought it would be in his best interests to cut the matter short."

"I am glad to have such a thoughtful man . . ."

"Here." He took her hand, slid the ring on, and kissed her again. Thomas then helped her into the car, placed both of her hands on top of the steering wheel, "Where people can see it," walked around to the other side of the car, and hopped in very cheerfully.

He looked at her for a minute. "Well, you'd be cheerful too."

She laughed and pulled the car around and headed back to Paradise. They were only a few miles from town, so the drive didn't take very long. Savannah slowed way down when they passed the sheriff and his men with their prisoner, and then sped up again.

She had begun to think about what Mrs. Fuller was going to say.

They pulled up in front of the boardinghouse, and
walked slowly and happily up the front steps, hand in
hand. When Thomas opened the door, they both saw
that Mrs. Fuller was sitting on Jack Smith's lap as they
came into the front parlor. She didn't jump up or react, but just continued there as though that was right
where she belonged, which it was.

"Well," said Thomas. "It appears that we are not
the *only* ones with this sort of news."

The wedding was six weeks later. The groom's eye
was much better, meaning that Mrs. Fuller no longer
thought he looked like the chaplain on a pirate ship.
And, as it happened, Mr. Machen was on a speaking
tour in the Northwest and agreed to officiate at the ceremony for his former student.

Savannah was no longer soaring the way that she
had been that day on the hill, but now that she knew
what flying was like, she had made a point to keep
at it. She had been aloft the entire six weeks, but she
made a point of keeping to respectable altitudes. She
had always been cheerful, but now . . .

But now. Now when the doors at the back of the
church swung open, and she fixed her eyes on Thomas,
and saw him standing there upright, in a stern glad-
ness, she felt like she was looking down at him from
the top of the emerald cloud of joy that surrounded that
rainbow in John's apocalypse. The brilliant notes of the
organ's glory had swirled down the aisle toward the

back of the church and washed around her feet like an incoming tide. The train of her dress and the organ music swirled around her feet together, gathering force. It continued to build until it picked her entirely up, and was carrying her to present her to the man at the center of the garden. God Himself was giving her away.

Thomas was getting closer, and so she knew she must be walking, but she had no sensation of her legs moving at all. She could feel the arm of the sheriff, a steady reassuring arm, but one that was no impediment at all to the joy. He had agreed to give her away, and when Thomas had asked him, he had said that it was the greatest honor he could ever remember receiving.

As she advanced down the aisle, Savannah knew herself to be beautiful, and there was no conceit in it anywhere, for the beauty belonged to another entirely. She was the glory of *another*. Her head was waiting for her at the front of the church, a dear, kind man. But she was not approaching him as though he were a head in need of feet; rather, her waiting head was bare and needed a crown.

The words of the ceremony were said, and that was part of the glory as well, even though it was all a blur. The words were familiar, and hence a comfort. The words were terrifying, and seemed weighted with a holy dread. The words were communal, and had been spoken by thousands and thousands of others, all resting in the grace of a covenant-keeping God.

The homily delivered by Mr. Machen was direct, inspiring, solid, meaty, and wise. Neither Thomas nor

K

Savannah remembered any of it from the wedding, but Mr. Machen was kind enough to leave a copy of it.

When it was over, Thomas and Savannah burst out of the church. The church bell was pealing as though its heart would break, and Savannah could barely hear it. She looked up because it felt just like mischievous spirits were running back and forth in the branches of the trees overhead. And perhaps they were.

POSTSCRIPT

"Well, I'm back," he said.

J.R.R. TOLKIEN, *THE RETURN OF THE KING*

The wedding reception was full and rich and happy, and so it was several hours before they were able to get away. Their plan was to go to Spokane by car, and to spend their honeymoon at the Davenport. When they finally left, they drove for about an hour, happily laughing and talking about all that had happened to them. "The lines have fallen for me in pleasant places," Thomas said. Savannah laughed. His lines were her lines.

Suddenly Savannah pointed past Thomas, out the left side of the car. "Look!" she said. They had come

247

out of a narrow valley, and a vista opened up to the west, and they saw the Palouse fields spread out before them for many miles. And there, above the fields, the sun was setting. It was in a tangled bank of orange and purple clouds, and it almost seemed as though the sun itself was in front of the clouds. "Look," Savannah said again. The sun almost seemed like the closest thing they could see.

Thomas saw a narrow dirt road wending off to the left, so he slowed down and quickly took it. "Let's just look at it for a few minutes," he said. They drove several hundred yards until the road abruptly ended on a small hillock. The highway behind them was out of sight. They got out of the car, completely and utterly alone. Ahead of them there was not a living soul for twenty miles, and it was probably close to that to the north and south. Behind them was the deserted highway.

They stood silently, watching the sun descend until the bottom of the circumference touched the horizon. Then they turned to go back to the car, and Thomas bent quickly and kissed Savannah quietly and touched her cheek.

"We should be there before dark," he said.

"Before the light dims," she replied.

THE END

Made in the USA
Columbia, SC
01 June 2020